Love on Tap

MOUNTAIN MEN OF CARIBOU CREEK BOOK 1

KALI HART

Love on Tap is a work of fiction. Names, characters, businesses, places, events, and incidents are either the products of the author's imagination or used in a fictitious manner. Any resemblance to actual persons, living or dead, or actual events is purely coincidental.

Copyright © 2022 by Kali Hart

ALL RIGHTS RESERVED. This book contains material protected under International and Federal Copyright Laws and Treaties. Any unauthorized reprint or use of this material is prohibited. No part of this book may be reproduced or transmitted in any form or by any electronic or mechanical means, including photocopying, recording, or by any information storage and retrieval systems, without express written permission from the author/publisher, except for the use of brief quotations in a book review.

CHAPTER 1

Riley

"Grandma Hattie, I *know* you're not trying to climb those stairs." My grandma, the most stubborn woman in the entire state of Alaska, freezes. Her injured leg, still wrapped in an ankle boot, hovers above a narrow stair. One I clearly remember forbidding her to climb only yesterday. Just as I've reminded her every day for the past week. "Whatever you need, I can go upstairs and grab it for you."

"I want my quilting room," she huffs, lowering her booted foot to the floor. "Can you bring *that* to me?"

I close my eyes, focus on my breathing, and count to ten. I've dealt with my share of ornery patients, but she's really taking the cake. Why didn't I consider her capacity for spunky hostility when I agreed to oversee her in-home rehab? "We've discussed this. Those stairs are too narrow. You can't make it up there without tilting your ankle. You know. The one you fractured. Are you *trying* to make it worse?"

Her stern expression softens, as does her tone of voice. "I haven't been up there in *two* weeks, Riley."

"I can bring some of your quilting supplies downstairs," I offer.

"It's not the same." Grandma Hattie's nearing eighty-five, but until she slipped on some wet gravel while wrangling a fish at the creek, no one would've guessed it. My grandpa is the first to tell anyone that she's a self-sufficient woman who insists on doing everything herself.

Her stubborn pride is the same reason she refused to stay in Anchorage or Fairbanks for physical therapy.

She's reminded me at least a dozen times since I temporarily moved into the guest room that she's lived in this house for fifty-five years and has no plans on leaving. And because grandpa loves her so much, he's not the best candidate for overseeing her rehab. He'd let her get away with murder.

It's why I volunteered to come home after nearly a decade away.

Well, not the *only* reason.

I push away the worrisome thoughts. They'll

haunt me plenty enough later tonight when I'm lying in bed, staring at the ceiling. Right now, the most important item on my agenda is to figure out how to deter Grandma Hattie from her mischief without it requiring constant supervision. Or an ankle monitor.

"Is it the *room* you miss?" I ask, glancing up the staircase staged along the back wall of the living room. It leads to only one room, and that's Grandma Hattie's quilting room.

"I need the ambiance to finish the baby blanket for Huck and Penny."

At the mention of my brother's name, an idea pops into my head. "What if I switched my room with the quilting room? That way your room would be on the main floor."

Grandma Hattie's eyebrows draw in and her expression screws up, like I might've just suggested she paint the living room logs pink. She *hates* pink. The room at the top of the stairs has been her quilting room ever since I can remember. "What about the view? And the lighting? You can't bring those down here. I can manage these stairs—"

I bolt in front of her so quickly she doesn't have a chance to plant her good leg on the bottom stair. "Not a chance."

"You're lucky your grandpa's still at work—"

"Hattie, what're you up to now?" The sound of Grandpa Harold's voice is music to my ears. He looks tired from another day at the shop. He retired a decade ago, but he refuses to admit it. He likes tinkering with cars, ATVs, and machinery. The guys enjoy his company and appreciate his expertise. I imagine it brings him the same joy that quilting brings Grandma Hattie.

"I want to get up to my quilting room. I need to finish my grandbaby's blanket."

Grandpa drops a hand on her shoulder, then looks to me. My heart melts at the sheer love in his eyes. He'd do anything for Grandma Hattie, and probably has over the six decades they've been together. "Still too early for stairs?" he asks.

Huck and Penny just announced that they were expecting last week. I bite down on my bottom lip, trying to swallow my frustration before I speak, hoping my tone betrays none of it. I know he means well. "The stairs are too narrow. It's not safe right now. If they were wider—"

"I've climbed these same stairs for fifty-five years," Grandma Hattie snaps back, the exasperation in her tone hinting that she might be near throwing the white flag in this fight. For now. But one night of rest and she'll be back at it again. I have to get this handled tonight. It can't wait.

"I suggested we switch her quilting room and my room," I explain to Grandpa. "I was about to run down to the brewery to see if Huck can stop by after work. I'll need help to move the heavy furniture." If I thought a text would be enough to get my brother here, I'd try that. But he's stubborn and thickheaded. Not to mention totally in love. I'll have to do this in person so he understands the seriousness of the situation or he'll blow me off.

When thoughts of Zac Ashburn drift in uninvited, I try to push them out. But it's not so easy. He's Huck's boss. It'd be impossible to talk to my brother and not run in to his best friend. I made up my mind when I bought the plane ticket that I'd be avoiding Zac as much as possible during my stay. So far, I've been successful. The last time I saw him, I was fifteen and planted a wet one right on his lips. Spoiler alert: he didn't kiss me back. In fact, he looked downright mortified. His expression is forever burned in my brain.

"I can help you," Grandpa offers.

I wish I could take him up on his offer, but he's not quite fit as a fiddle anymore. And some of the furniture is crazy heavy. I don't need two grandparents down for the count. "I know you can, Grandpa. But someone needs to keep an eye on our wild child. She's out of control today. Maybe you could take her out for a drive or something?"

Grandma Hattie flutters her eyelashes at Grandpa, feigning innocence. I know he doesn't buy it, but he plants a kiss on her forehead anyway. Damn them and their cuteness. I'd kill to find someone to spend a lifetime with. Someone who'd look at me like I hung the moon in their sky, even when I'm a hundred. But when it comes to men, I have a knack at picking all the wrong ones.

"Hattie, you might like your quilts down here for a change. A different view could give you more...inspiration." Grandpa's always had a way with words. He can get through to Grandma Hattie like no one else can. He looks back to me. "Why don't you go see if you can grab Huck. I'll keep my sweetheart out of trouble. I'm craving a piece of Rose's blueberry pie."

I don't dare waste a second, even if the thought of seeing Zac Ashburn again after all these years makes me excited and nauseous at the same time. Of course, the nausea could be from something else entirely. *What a mess.* "I'll be right back. No funny business, Grandma Hattie."

"I assure you, the only funny business will be later,

behind closed doors," Grandpa says, effectively moving my feet right out the door before he can say something that'll scar me for life.

If only Grandma Hattie's ornery behavior was my biggest problem, life might not be so bad. But the shitty reality is she's the least of them. I back the car out of the driveway, hoping Zac called in sick today. But I don't have that kind of luck.

CHAPTER 2

Zac

"One Caribou Creek Pale Ale and one Caribou Creek Pilsner," I say to the couple next in line at the bar, sliding two glasses to them. The brewery's been busier than usual for a Monday. I know it's good for business. A business I'm part owner of with my brothers. My livelihood depends on its continued success. But I'd be lying if I said I wasn't stealing glances at the clock, willing time to go by faster.

I let Decker, one our part time bartenders, help the next person in line and return my attention back to the couple seated at the end of the bar.

I'm still shocked as hell that James Devano, playboy coast guard pilot and sworn lifelong bachelor, is here with a woman. He doesn't bring flings to town, or so he's told me. Maybe after all these years of resisting, a woman's finally got her hooks into him. From the interaction I've watched between them so far, I think she'll be good for him. She doesn't take any of his shit and isn't afraid to give it right back.

The ache I feel in my own chest is surprising. I push it away. I don't know that I have any business getting tangled up with a woman. Some days my head's a bigger mess than others. The flashbacks from Afghanistan plague me without warning for no fucking reason at all. Today has been one of those days. I yearn for the solitude of my cabin a couple miles from town. Out there, I can split wood until I chase them away.

"Don't rush me," the woman says playfully to James, bringing me back to the present.

Earlier, I set her up with a sample platter and took my time explaining the flavor pallet of each of the six brews we offer—Ben, my oldest brother who's in charge of sales and marketing, would have my head if I didn't. Sometimes he takes his job too seriously.

She's halfway through her samples before I realize I haven't offered James a drink. *Fuck, where* is *my head today?*

I turn to him. "Do you—"

"Is he here?" a woman demands, drawing my

attention away from James and his date. I suck in a breath, prepared to lock my friendly smile into place so I can politely put *her* in her place. We don't tolerate rudeness or assholes at our brewery. It's an automatic invitation out the door. But when I lift my gaze, I'm stunned into silence.

Dark auburn curls cascade over the front of her shoulders. My mouth suddenly dries. In her skinny jeans and muted green top, it's impossible not to notice and appreciate her curves. But it's those intense blue eyes that capture my attention and refuse to let it go. *Riley Kohl?* The last time I saw her, she was just a kid.

But there's nothing *kid* about her now.

Not even close.

She folds both arms over her chest, unwilling to offer me a smile. It's been well over a decade since I last saw my buddy's little sister. If it weren't for those eyes, I don't know that I would've recognized her. I'd heard she was in town. Nothing stays a secret in Caribou Creek. But I haven't run into her until now. And she does *not* look happy to see me. I can't figure out why that bothers me so much.

"Huck," she prompts snappishly, as if I'm not an old friend. "Is he here?"

"Your brother's cleaning out the fermentation tanks."

"How long will that take?"

I'm determined to rid her of that scowl. I can't imagine why she's wearing it. She used to follow Huck and me around all the time when we were growing up. The three of us were thick as thieves. "Long enough for you to sit and have a drink."

"I'm in a hurry," she says, glancing around the brewery. I suspect the last time she saw the place, my grandparents were still running it. My brothers and I have made a lot of improvements since taking over. The rustic tin walls might be the only detail we didn't change.

"What are you drinking? We have six different—"

"I'm not." She moves to the edge of the counter and stretches up on tiptoe, as if that'll help her see over the saloon doors to the back. But they're too tall for her short frame. "Can you hurry him up or something? I have to get back before Grandma Hattie gets into more trouble."

"How is she?" I ask, recalling she fractured her ankle a couple of weeks ago.

"Stubborn as ever."

I can't seem to keep my gaze from raking over her

curves. I haven't felt this drawn to a woman in ... ever. *Shit. Play it cool, Zac. Your head's a fucking mess. That's the only reason you're having these thoughts about Huck's little sister.* "You came back to help her out for a while?"

"I'm overseeing her at-home rehab, but I'm not staying. I'm headed back to Orlando as soon as she doesn't need me anymore." She reaches into her purse and pulls out a ten-dollar bill. Slapping it on the counter, she says, "Give me an amber."

"Good choice," I say, refusing to take her money as I fill a glass and wonder what her life is like in Orlando. She always used to talk about leaving Caribou Creek and moving somewhere bigger. A city that never slept. But part of me thought she'd always end up back here. I thought all three of us would. "The amber's our most popular," I add, handing the glass to her instead of sliding it over. Which ends up being a big fucking mistake. A simple graze of our fingertips as we exchange the glass sends a jolt of electricity up my arm. *What the hell?*

Riley flinches. I give myself a whole second to consider that she felt it too. But she's looking at the glass of amber like it's poison and she doesn't know how it got there.

"Are you—"

"Um, I'll be right back." She sets the glass on the counter and hurries toward the restroom in the corner.

I force myself to shift my attention back to James, remembering he requested a to-go order to take back to North Haven. Luckily Decker has his wits about him and boxed it all up. "Sorry about that man," I say to James, setting the wooden crate filled with six packs of the J-Squad's favorite brews. Though I try my damnedest to focus on my customers, I can't help but glance toward the restrooms, wondering if Riley's okay.

"Be careful with that one," James says, handing over his credit card.

So much for being discreet. "Don't I know it."

As James and his date leave, Riley reappears at the bar. I'm relieved she's not looking green, but still confused about her suddenly running off. But she doesn't waste any time explaining herself. "Is Huck done yet? I need his help moving furniture at—"

"Dude!" Huck bursts through the saloon doors, waving his phone. "She got it! Penny got the gig!"

It takes me a few seconds to remember what he's talking about, which is embarrassing considering he hasn't shut up about it all week. His wife, Penny, auditioned to open for a major concert in Anchorage. Though she doesn't sing professionally and doesn't want that lifestyle, her voice could win any music competition out there. "That's great, man! When is it?"

Huck looks up from his phone, a guilty expression spreading across his features. "This weekend. They want us in Anchorage tomorrow morning for press, rehearsals, and all that. I'll run it by Wes. Make sure I can take the time off —"

"No need." I'm not giving either one of my brothers the opportunity to turn down the last-minute request. Wes, the brew master, would probably approve even though he's shorthanded right now. But Ben will be a pain in the ass. Better for me to handle this now and deal with the repercussions later. "I'll talk to him."

"You can't leave yet," Riley says.

"Oh hey, sis. Didn't see you there." Huck's wearing his goofy, cupid-hit-me-in-the-ass grin that he's had on since he met Penny. I'm happy as hell for him, but I have to admit, I'm a little jealous. Huck didn't come home from Afghanistan with the same trauma I did. He had his whole heart to give. "Sorry, I have to go straight home. Penny needs help packing."

"I need help switching Grandma Hattie's quilting room with my room. She's been trying to sneak upstairs again. Do you want her to fall and break her other ankle? Or worse, her *neck*?" Riley folds both arms over her chest again, tapping her foot. When did she learn to put up such thick walls? Why did she? I feel something inside me bristle. *What asshole did this to her?*

"I can help," I hear myself offer before I've had a moment to think it through.

"You sure, man?" Huck asks.

"I'm free tonight. It's no problem at all." I meet Riley's eyes for the first time since Huck erupted on the scene. I'm afraid my buddy'll catch me staring at his little sister like she's a dessert. A dessert I yearn to taste more by the minute. "That work for you?" I ask her, hoping like hell I sound calm and in control of my breathing. My pulse is another matter.

"How soon can you come over?"

"Give me an hour?"

"See, there you go," Huck says. "Problem solved."

"It'd go faster with all three of us," Riley adds, but it's no use. Huck's already turned his back and disappeared through the saloon doors. She stares at the swinging doors for several seconds before turning her baby blue gaze on me. "You might be in over your head. Grandma Hattie's out of control."

Riley adjusts her purse strap on her shoulder and about faces, abandoning her untouched beer. The sway of her hips as she marches toward the door causes my dick to twitch against my zipper. I discreetly stare at her amazing ass. My fingers itch with yearning to sink into her plump flesh. Yeah, I might be in more trouble than I realized.

CHAPTER 3

Riley

"You good?" Zac calls from the middle of the staircase, sounding not nearly winded enough for all the trips we've been making between the two rooms. The mattress wobbles in my grasp, threatening to topple over the railing and into the living room. Though it wouldn't flatten my grandparents if it fell—Grandpa managed to convince Grandma Hattie to grab some pie from the local diner while we made the switch—it would definitely destroy a lamp or two.

"Remind me to get even with Huck when he gets back," I grumble, knowing my threat is empty. With how lost Huck seemed for the last few years, I'm happy he found a good woman. Penny's amazing. The only qualm I have about him leaving for Anchorage last minute is that the timing sucks.

"I would've rounded up more help, but we couldn't spare anyone else tonight."

Dammit, why does he have to be so endearing? I want to stay mad at Zac. Staying mad at him keeps my embarrassing teenage crush from resurfacing. I might not be the same awkward fifteen-year-old with braces anymore, but I'm not exactly a super model. I'm sure Zac gets hit on by every single female tourist who visits the CARIBOU CREEK BREWERY. For all I know, his bedroom is a revolving door.

"It's all good," I say, practically grunting the words. "We're almost finished. You'll be able to leave soon."

"I don't mind helping, Riley."

I ignore his words so I can't read into his tone and focus on maneuvering the pillowtop mattress into the oddly shaped room with random angled ceilings. We position it against the bedframe and let it fall.

Once it's in place, I drop on to the mattress and sigh. "Remind me to never buy a pillowtop mattress unless I'm paying someone else to lug it around. It's like sleeping on a cloud, but dammit this thing's heavy."

Zac rubs out a kink in his neck, but I pretend not

to notice. The last thing I need to think about is those hands on my body. Or sex. Sex leads to bad decisions and just complicates everything in the end. No matter what I find out when I'm finally brave enough to face things, I need to avoid sex for at least a year. Maybe longer.

"Never slept on a pillowtop before," Zac admits. "But after a year at a time on a cot, any mattress is better."

"You have to try it," I insist, patting a spot next to me before I think it through. Too late to revoke the invitation now without sounding like a jerk. Once upon a time, we were just innocent kids who wouldn't have thought twice about lying on the same bed. "Just lie down for a minute. I'm not going to bite." *Unless you want me to.*

Zac sits on the edge of the mattress, keeping a healthy distance from me, and slowly leans back. "Hey, this is pretty nice."

"Right?"

He props his hands behind his head and stares up at the ceiling. "I might have to get one of these."

For a moment, it feels just like old times. Before I developed my embarrassing crush on him, spending time with Zac was normal. It was always Huck, Zac, and me when we were younger. "Do you remember that time we thought we could catch the moose that was stealing raspberries out of Mrs. Johnson's garden?" I ask, wondering what else he remembers.

"You mean the time when Huck smashed half her raspberries patch because the moose decided to chase *us* out of it?" Zac's chuckle is soft, little more than a puff of air. I feel my nipples harden, as if his breath is on them and not lost to the space above us.

"I'll never forget how *big* that thing was," I say, adding my laughter to his, remembering how fearless I used to be. It almost makes me sad now. With one bad decision after another, I have a hard time trusting myself these days. I live a very boring life outside of work. Any time I seem to stray from that safe, boring routine, I tend to find trouble.

"Huck's just lucky the damn thing didn't flatten him like a pancake. Your mom would've killed us if he got trampled." Zac turns his head, his brown eyes meeting mine. This close, I can see the familiar gold flecks in his irises. "How *is* your mom, anyway?"

"Remarried. Again." Mom moved to Arizona the minute I left for college. She'd moved to Caribou Creek when she married my dad, but he passed away when I was only nine. Didn't take long before Mom was itching to leave. She never really felt at home in Alaska. "Still in Arizona."

Zac shifts his body until he's lying on his side. He props his head in a hand. For some reason the way he's looking at me is making me feel more vulnerable than I already did. Which is the only reason my own gaze goes rouge, dropping to places it has no business dropping. Wetness pools between my legs as I take in all the hard muscles suffocating beneath his tight t-shirt. I wonder what he's hiding in those jeans... "What about you, Riley?"

I clear my throat and pretend to fix my hair, certain I've been caught. "What about me?"

He pokes me near the shoulder hard enough to rock me, like he used to do when we were kids. Except the simple sensation of his touch has every nerve ending in my body on high alert. "Don't play dumb. You're better than that."

I'm not about to tell Zac Ashburn of all people that I might be pregnant. That the very sight of a glass of Caribou Creek Amber earlier freaked me out so much that I ran to the bathroom, afraid I might throw up—which I thankfully didn't. Or that I'm too chicken to pee on a stick and find out the truth. "I'm a physical therapist. In Orlando."

He rolls his eyes at me, and for some reason the carefree gesture makes my pulse double. So much for my teenage crush staying buried in the past where it belongs. It takes an embarrassing amount of restraint to keep my hands to myself. Damn the Army. It was obviously good to him and all those delicious muscles. "I already knew that."

"I live in an apartment with a lake view." I omit the detail about the cement factory on the opposite side of said lake, which is why rent is dirt cheap. "Thought about getting a cat."

Zac stares at me so intently it makes me feel naked. Uncomfortable. Afraid that if he keeps searching, he'll discover all my secrets. I didn't come home to fall for him all over again. Yet, in a matter of hours I'm already yearning to have him back in my life. I don't like this one bit.

"There's that look again," Zac says.

"What look?"

"The scowl you gave me earlier at the brewery. Did I do something to upset you?"

I'm not about to tell him that he's the reason I've avoided Caribou Creek for all these years. He's always been my kryptonite. If only I had a legitimate reason to be mad at him. But I'm only mad at myself. "Do you honestly not remember?"

"Remember what?"

Oh god. He's going to make me say it out loud. *Abort, Riley. Just abort.* "Never mind."

LOVE ON TAP

Zac scoots closer, making it impossible not to feel the warmth radiating from his body. The scent of his woodsy cologne rushes my senses. *That's new.* "Riley, what is it? You know you can tell me anything, right?" The familiar words from our childhood days create an ache in my heart. The tingling in my nipples is caused by something else entirely.

"You don't remember that I—"

"Riley? You home?" Grandma Hattie calls up the stairs, causing me to catapult off the bed as if she'd been standing in the doorway. Never mind that Zac and I weren't doing anything inappropriate. Or that we're both full-grown adults. "I brought you some pie."

"Coming." I don't wait for Zac to follow. I bolt down the stairs, convincing myself I need to keep Grandma Hattie from making another attempt to climb them. She *has* been extra spunky these past couple of days. That's totally the reason I'm in a hurry. It has nothing to do with getting space from Zac Ashburn.

"You still like apple, right?" Grandma Hattie asks, handing me a Styrofoam container.

"Still my favorite. Thank—"

"Zac, how lovely to see you," Grandma Hattie gushes, her attention one hundred percent shifting

23

from me, her only granddaughter, to Zac. She always did like him the best out of the three of us. Probably because he's not blood related. "Riley, share your piece of pie with him."

"What?"

"I don't need any pie, ma'am." Zac saunters down the stairs, as if he has all the time in the world. As if we didn't almost share a moment up there. Not a trace of guilt etched on his perfectly chiseled face. "Thank you, though."

"Don't you *dare* call me ma'am," Grandma Hattie scolds playfully. "Ma'am will *always* be my mother, no matter how close to a hundred I get. It's Hattie."

"Yes ma'am—Hattie."

"Zac helped me move the furniture," I explain. "Huck's tied up."

"I heard!" Grandma Hattie's entire face lights up. "I hope they play that concert on the internet contraption. I'd love to hear her sing."

Zac and I share a quick amused glance that *should* be completely innocent. But the droves of butterflies erupting in my belly say otherwise. I'd swear there was a trace of heat in his dark eyes. Except it's more likely my overactive imagination is at work again. "I'll ask Huck if they're live streaming it," I say to Grandma Hattie.

But there's a dangerous twinkle in her eyes as they bounce between Zac and me. *Oh no. No, no. Down, Grandma Hattie!* "Zac, I can whip you up something to eat if you're hungry. Can't let all your help go unappreciated."

"I can't stay," Zac says, moving around me to get to Grandma Hattie. The brush of his shoulder against mine makes me a bit dizzy. Or maybe it's that delicious cologne. When I get back to Orlando, I'm buying a bottle and spraying it on my pillow. It'll be the closest thing I get to having a man in my bed for the foreseeable future.

Zac wraps Grandma Hattie in a hug. "You take it easy now," he says to her. "Don't give your granddaughter too much grief." He slips me a wink that causes those pesky butterflies in my belly to do loop-de-loops. "She's only looking out for you."

Shoving both hands in the back pockets of my jeans, I watch the first boy I ever had a crush on slip out the front door. Maybe in a different set of circumstances, this could be the start of something. But with the tangled mess my life has become, I can't entertain those thoughts.

No matter how badly I want to.

CHAPTER 4

Zac

I wake in a cold sweat, panting heavily and stomach in knots. The images from my nightmare flash faintly behind my eyelids. Memories from Afghanistan I'd rather forget. "Fuck," I mutter, angrily shoving the covers aside and hopping out of bed for the shower.

After the military, I did the responsible thing and sought help to deal with the plague of war. I thought I had a handle on it. For years, I've lived a mostly normal existence. But these past few months have dredged up some of my more traumatic memories, and I can't seem to put my finger on why.

I turn the water on and stand beneath the stream, willing my mind to wander *anywhere* else.

I'm not going to bite.

Though desperate to replace the warzone visions, I'm shocked that Riley Kohl's voice pulls me out of my darkness. I blink for an extra-long moment, allowing her sweet image to replace the horrific ones. My heartrate instantly slows as a calm settles over me.

I try to reconcile the impossibility of it. Why *her*?

She's familiar. That's all. Her dark auburn hair in its long, lazy curls. The golden highlights framing her pretty face. Those startling blue eyes that have only gotten bluer with time. Her lips curl into a mischievous smile.

But the image doesn't stop there.

Oh no.

My wild imagination is clearly on a mission to distract me to the fullest.

I squeeze my eyes shut, resting my forehead against the tile wall as the hot water runs over my back. My steady heart rate begins to climb once again, but for an entirely different reason this time. I allow the forbidden fantasy to unfold. It's as the camera lens that was focused solely on her face zooms out.

Riley stands before me in those skinny jeans and a sleeveless top that she begins to unbutton. Dear fucking god. I grip my cock—the fucker's already half hard—and begin to stroke it as my fantasy girl undoes another button. I'm teased by the hard nipples poking through the fabric. Another button undone reveals she's not wearing a bra. When did her tits get so *big*?

I stroke faster, shocked at how quickly my release finds me.

Hot ropes of cum shoot onto the tile wall before fantasy Riley works the last button of her top.

I'm panting heavily as my eyes pop back open, not sure what the fuck I should be feeling. I'm relieved that I was able to ward off the unwanted memories from my Army days. But to have them so easily wiped away with forbidden fantasies of my buddy's little sister isn't exactly great news.

I can't get involved with Riley.

I'm slipping on a t-shirt when I hear a knock on the front door. I live a couple of miles outside of town for a reason. To avoid people. It has to be one of my brothers. Probably Ben, who's pissed I let Huck take off without clearing it with him first. He makes the schedule, and not consulting him when there's changes really gets his boxers in a twist.

Pulling the door open, I launch right into my defense. "Ben, he didn't have time—"

"Not Ben."

I drop my gaze lower and find Riley Kohl standing on my doorstep, holding out a covered baking pan. My dick twitches in my pants, completely unaware that the shower was pure fantasy. Something that can never be realized in reality. "What's this?"

"Homemade caramel brownies. Grandma Hattie insisted." She holds them out again. "Can I come in for a sec?"

"Uh, sure." I step back, allowing Riley inside. Because we're friends. It'd be rude not to invite a friend inside.

"Wow, this place is amazing." She tilts her head all the way up, admiring the vaulted log ceiling. "No way! You have a caribou antler chandelier. You always talked about having one when we were kids."

"You remembered." Finally, I free her of the brownies and carry them to the kitchen. She follows me, not shy about looking around.

"Of course I remember. The three of us used to sit on that old fishing dock, imagining what our lives would be like. What kind of houses we'd live in. What kind of cars we'd drive."

"Did you get your Mustang?"

"I did," she says, running her fingertips along my black quartz countertops. "But some jackass made a left turn on a red and t-boned me. Totaled it a week after I bought it." She lifts her baby blue gaze to me, and I nearly forget how to speak. I blame the unsolicited fantasy in the shower. One I'll have to take with me to the grave. "Do you *really* not remember what I did the day you and Huck left for basic training?"

This has to be why she's been mad at me since she saw me in the brewery last night. But for the life of me, I haven't been able to figure out what I did all those years ago that's warranted her anger. "I'm sorry. I don't." I focus on the baking pan and help myself to a brownie. After my first bite, I realize I didn't offer one to Riley. But she turns it down.

"You don't remember me *kissing* you?"

I freeze at the words, instant panic flooding me. Did I do something that immature and stupid back then? "I kissed you?"

"No, *you* didn't." She covers her face with both hands and groans into them. "You know what, forget I said anything. I need to get going. If Grandma Hattie tried to get rid of me this morning, there's a reason. She's probably up to no good."

Riley's at the front door before I can register that she's trying to make an escape. I'm forced to run after her, catching the door with a firm hand before it closes. "Riley, wait."

She stops three feet from the front stoop, looking as mortified as I've ever seen her. "I really thought you remembered. I've just been wanting to apologize. Sorry I said anything. Just go back to forgetting—"

"If I ever get the chance to kiss you again, I promise I won't forget it. I doubt you will either." The bold words are out before I make the clear decision to speak them. I could blame my forbidden shower fantasy or a shitty night of sleep. But it's more than either of those things that's fueling the urgent need to bring a smile back to her perfect lips.

"You shouldn't say things you don't mean."

I'm prevented from a response because my oldest brother chooses *that* moment to tear into my driveway like he's being chased by a SWAT team. He's not, of course. He's too perfect to be in trouble with the law. He's probably just impatient and probably about to rip me a new asshole for giving Huck time off without consulting him.

"Riley—" But she's already in her grandpa's old beater truck, backing out of the driveway. Huck and I taught her how to drive in that truck. I stare after her. *Did she really kiss me and I don't remember?*

"I thought we had an agreement," Ben says, looking as pissed off as a taunted bull moose. "All time off goes through *me*."

"I'm sorry," I say, laying on the sarcasm thickly. I fold my arms over my chest and lean back against the door jamb. "I forgot Wes and I appointed you King of the Brewery at our last owner's meeting."

"Stop being a jackass." Ben looks over his shoulder. "What was Riley Kohl doing here?"

"Why do you care?"

"Fuck man. Do I have to remind you about *all* the rules?"

After the shitty night of sleep I had for the twentieth or thirtieth time in a row—I've lost count—I'm in no mood for Ben's shit today. "Did you really come here to lecture me about time off?" Though I wouldn't put it past him, I suspect he would've waited until I got to the brewery today to say something if there wasn't another reason he was here.

"You can't dip your pen in company ink, Zac."

I stare at him like he's grown two heads. "Riley doesn't work for us." Why that seems the more important detail to clear up and *not* that I didn't sleep with her, I don't know. Even if Riley were staying and Huck was cool with it, I'm too broken inside. Riley deserves better than the fractures pieces of me I could offer her.

"But her brother does. You think that through at all?"

My head is pounding, which isn't unusual after the nightmares. But it's getting much worse with Ben in my face. I haven't told either of my brothers that the PTSD is back. I don't need them monitoring me like I'm a bomb that could go off at any time. "Tell me why you're really here or I'm going back inside and locking the door."

"Because you don't answer your fucking phone," he grumbles. "Supply truck came a day early and kegs need to be cleaned. Since you sent Huck to Anchorage without telling anyone, you get to pick up the slack. Get your ass down to the brewery an hour ago."

"Let me grab my keys. I'm right behind you." I slam the door closed before he can get another jerkish jab in. It's pointless to remind Ben that he's not the boss. The three of us make decisions together and have equal sway in our family-owned company. I also don't need any more lecturing about Riley Kohl. Should I have made that comment about kissing her? Probably not. But would I take it back given the chance? No way in hell.

CHAPTER 5

Riley

"What do you mean I can't stay here?" I watch Grandma Hattie pull down wine glasses from the cupboard near the sink, ready to pounce if she drops something. Maybe I've been hovering too much for the past couple of days. But it gives me an excuse to stay in. To avoid Zac Ashburn and his dangerously tempting words. "It's just a bridge game."

Grandpa Harold lets out a good laugh as he enters the kitchen. "Just a bridge game," he mumbles, shaking his head. He sets a hand on Grandma Hattie's shoulder and kisses her forehead. "You've been gone too many years, pumpkin," he says to me. He redirects his attention to his wife. "Need anything before I head to poker night?"

"Yes." Grandma Hattie points a glare at me. "Get rid of my parole officer. What will the ladies think if she's hovering around me all night, watching my every move? It'll throw me off my game. I can't let them smell weakness."

I hide a laugh behind my hand, realizing I'm going to miss Grandma Hattie's spunkiness once I return to Orlando. I make a mental note to get over my damn self, and my pitiful crush, so I can visit once in a while. While I still can. *If they don't disown me first.*

I *should* head to the grocery store or gas station and get a pregnancy test. Rip the band-aid off. But in a town as small as Caribou Creek, there's no way I can make such a purchase without a rumor spreading like wildfire. "Since you won't invite me to play cards, just where am I supposed to go?"

Before Grandma Hattie can list off some suggestions, a knock at the kitchen door turns all our heads. Her bridge ladies aren't supposed to show up for at least an hour. Huck and Penny are out of town—

"Zac, come on in!" Grandma Hattie wraps her arms around his waist, unashamedly resting her head against the middle of his torso since she's not tall enough to reach his hard chest. Completely unaware that my pulse has tripled in a single breath. I had hoped the space would help me get my head on straight when it comes to Zac Ashburn. But clearly, it's had the opposite effect. My damn nipples are pebbled in seconds, reminding me of the promise that left his lips. One about a kiss neither of us would forget.

"I brought back your brownie pan," he says, lifting it as evidence.

"You're just in time."

"Oh no," I chime in before this gets any crazier. "Grandma Hattie, don't you *dare*." I should've seen it the other night when that dangerous twinkle was dancing in her eyes. She saw *something* when she looked between Zac and me. The sly devil is trying to play matchmaker.

"Are you busy tonight, Zac?" she asks.

Grandpa Harold plants another kiss on her temple, throws me a wink, and slips out the door. Leaving me to fight my own battle. *Gee thanks*.

"Got the evening free, actually. Did you need me to help move more furniture?"

"Not tonight. The ladies are coming over for bridge." She loops an arm through his and subtly guides him in my direction. "Which is why I need Riley to leave. All her fussing is sweet, but it'll ruin my concentration. I'm on a winning streak."

"Are you sure this is a *bridge* game?" I ask, highly

suspicious that these old ladies are gathering to gamble. Maybe that's why Grandma Hattie wants me gone. She doesn't want me to find the poker chips or black jack table. "Never mind. I don't want to know," I add, holding up my hands. "Grandma Hattie, can I really trust you not to overdo it? Your ankle—"

"Rose'll keep me out of trouble. She was a nurse before she bought the diner, you know." Somehow, she's finagled herself and Zac to within arm's reach of me. She pats my arm fondly. "We all have former lives, you know. She's on her way over right now."

"Sounds like your grandma has everything handled," Zac says, wearing a half smile that threatens to undo me. I haven't been able to stop thinking about what he said when I left his place yesterday. It's not enough that my traitorous body can't keep itself under control at the sight of him. But I've been fantasizing about that kiss. One that wouldn't leave me embarrassed and hiding until he left town.

"You're going to entertain me?" I challenge.

"I think that's a grand idea!" Grandma Hattie's eyes are twinkling again.

"I have an idea," Zac says, holding out his hand for mine. "Do you trust me?"

I stare at his hand for several long beats before

flicking my gaze up to his. "The last time you asked me that, I ended up covered in mud from head to toe."

"But you had fun, right?"

The memory of me holding onto him tight as he four-wheeled it through the bumpiest, muddiest trails in history still warms me from the inside out. It was the day I realized I had a crush on him. I could've been covered in moose crap and still been stupidly happy. "I don't want to get dirty tonight," I say, pointing a stern finger at him.

Zac grabs my hand, causing tingles to skitter up my arm. "No promises."

"Zac!"

A knock at the door announces the arrival of Rose Clayton, owner of THE CARIBOU CREEK DINER. "Out you go!" Grandma Hattie ushers us both toward the door. "Don't come back until the stars come out."

I'm two steps out the back door before it dawns on me. "The stars don't come out this time of year—"

Zac drapes an arm over my shoulders, guiding me away from the house. Something he's done hundreds of times in our youth. But this is the first time electricity zings up and down my body like a damn lightning storm is happening inside of me. I steal a quick glance at his lips, wondering if I'll get that second chance to try them out tonight. Wondering if a kiss, now that we're older, will lead to more.

"Where are we going?" I ask as he holds the passenger door of his truck open.

He winks at me, causing those pesky stomach butterflies to throw a dance party. "Now what fun would it be if I spoiled the surprise?"

CHAPTER 6
Zac

Though I told myself I only stopped by Hattie's to drop off the brownie pan, I knew it was a lie. I haven't seen Riley since yesterday morning, when she practically ran away at the mention of a kiss I still don't remember. Her absence since has left me feeling restless and antsy, and I don't like it one bit. The need to see her was too overwhelming to ignore.

"The old boat dock is still here?" she asks, her eyes lighting up when I pull up to the edge of a graveled area. A spot where the three of us used to drop our bikes. We used to come out here all the time when we were kids. We'd fish, not that we caught anything, and waste an entire day eating junk food we snuck out of their mom's pantry. My favorite part was always the daydreaming. Our plans. Our big what ifs.

"It is."

"Is it safe?"

"Yes." I cut the ignition and push open my door. "You coming?"

"If I fall through a rotted board and get wet—"

"Though I wouldn't mind seeing you soaked from head from toe, the boards are new. I fixed it up a couple summers ago." I close the door and head toward the dock, leaving her to catch up. Putting me far enough in front of her so I can't see her expression. I'm left to wonder if she caught what I was really saying.

"Why would you do that?" she asks, stopping at the point where the grass meets the wooden planks. "*How* did you do it and not get shot? Wait, is Old Man Jenkins...*dead*?" She gasps, her wide eyes and panicked expression so damn cute. It makes me yearn for things I've convinced myself I don't deserve.

"He retired. Moved to Charleston."

"Who owns it now?"

At the dock, I turn and look back at Riley. She hesitates at the edge, as if she can't quite trust she won't end up in the water if she dares to join me. It gives me an extra moment to discreetly rake my gaze up and down her curvy body. Damn, she's filled out in all the right ways. What I wouldn't give to watch her unbutton that top and reveal her bountiful tits for my viewing pleasure. The part of me that knows I shouldn't be thinking these things about Huck's little sister has apparently checked out tonight. "I do."

"*You* own it?"

"Old Man Jenkins sold it to me when he left town."

She takes a couple cautious steps forward, picking up her pace when she accepts it's safe. "How could you afford it?"

Old Man Jenkins got dozens of solid offers over the years, but he wasn't as interested in money as he was in selling it to someone who appreciated the land. On each deployment, I tucked away as much money as I could. "There's a lot you don't know about me, Riley Kohl. That happens when you disappear for fourteen years."

"You weren't in Caribou Creek the whole time," she says, narrowing her eyes at me.

I kick off my shoes and sit on the edge of the dock. I pat the space beside me, but Riley doesn't sit. "I don't bite," I say, repeating her words from the other night. "Unless you want me to."

She rolls her eyes at me before quickly turning

away. But she's not fast enough to hide the redness creeping up her neck at my words. The one thing that's been undeniable since we laid eyes on each other in the brewery Monday night is the chemistry that's crackling between us. A pull so strong that physical distance will no longer be enough to keep us apart. I know she feels it too. It's the heat dancing in her eyes. We'll crave each other no matter how many miles or obstacles separate us.

Finally, Riley kicks off her sandals and joins me, dangling her toes in the water. I feel her tension as if it were my own. Something is troubling her. It'll trouble me too unless I can help her. But Riley Kohl is as stubborn as they come, second only to her grandma. "Did you accomplish any of those dreams you dreamed up out here? Besides the Mustang."

"I don't have the million-dollar mansion overlooking the ocean," she admits, offering a weak smile to the creek. "I didn't marry Justin Bieber and have his babies. Thirty was my cut-off. Considering that's only a few months away, it's probably too late to accomplish that dream. Unless I'm unknowingly carrying his triplets—"

She stops abruptly and clears her throat. Trouble flickers in her eyes. Never in my life have I wanted to bring someone peace as much as I want that for Riley.

I'd endure a thousand years of war nightmares if only she could smile without reservation. Whatever is eating at her, it's more than some kiss I don't remember. It's much more. "Riley—"

"What about you? You obviously took over the family brewery with your brothers. You always talked about doing that."

I lean back on my hands, daring to slide one closer to her. Not touching, but close enough that I can feel the heat of her dancing against my thumb. It takes every ounce of restraint I have not to run my hand up her arm. What I wouldn't give to caress every inch of her naked body and commit the feeling to memory. "We took over ownership from my grandparents three and a half years ago when they decided to retire and move south. They live in a bungalow on a white sandy beach, just like Grandma always wanted. And Grandpa gets to fish all day, every day."

I dare to graze my thumb against hers, caressing with a feather's gentleness. She stares down at my hand but doesn't pull hers away. "Sounds like it all worked out, then."

"Yeah, I guess it did."

"Is it hard? Not having them in Caribou Creek?" She lifts her gaze to mine and dammit if my pulse doesn't double on the spot. Those baby blues, filled with compassion, reach inside me to depths I never thought a person could penetrate.

"I still have my brothers." I slide my hand atop hers. She turns her hand, offering me her palm as our fingers thread together. My dick twitches against my zipper, reminding me of the many forbidden fantasies starring Riley Kohl and very little clothing. Fantasies that have been on repeat since the morning I stroked myself in the shower to her image. "You're still going back to Orlando?"

"My whole life is there."

I scoot closer to her, resting our joined hands on her thigh. "Your job. Your apartment. Your theoretical cat."

"His name is Mr. Whiskers."

"How original." My gaze drops to her soft lips, wondering why the hell I can't remember her kissing me all those years ago. Not that it could've led anywhere. I was eighteen, leaving for basic training. She was fifteen and my buddy's little sister. But now that we're older, the three-year age gap means nothing. Everything about this moment feels...natural. As if we've been here a thousand times before. As if we'll be here a thousand more.

"It's *my* theoretical cat. I can name him whatever I want."

I dare to lean closer, reaching for a stray lock of hair the breeze is set on teasing. I tuck it behind her ear. I should pull my hand away. But I've already come too far to turn back now. I know there'll be some complications with Huck, but we'll work them out when he gets back. I have to have Riley Kohl for my own. I need her as badly as I need oxygen. I know I'm a broken man, but maybe what I need to heal is sitting beside me, parting her lips in anticipation.

"Ready for that kiss you'll never forget?" I ask in a heated whisper, tucking my fingers beneath her jaw and tugging her closer. I don't give her a chance to answer the question before I brush my lips against hers. I pause, giving her a moment to pull away. But she doesn't. She reaches for my cheek, tugging me closer.

The kiss deepens as our lips press harder together. I thread my fingers into her hair, certain she'll give me shit later for messing up her ponytail. I run my tongue between her lips, begging for entry she willingly grants.

She softly moans into my mouth as our tongues do a dance.

Before Riley Kohl showed back up in Caribou Creek, I never would've guessed she was The One. But suddenly it makes sense why it never worked out with anyone else. I can blame my war trauma all I want, but deep down I knew something was missing with the women I dated. *She* was missing.

With one kiss, I know my fate with Riley is sealed. There'll never be another for me. The sudden realization should scare me more than any IED ever did, but instead it has the opposite effect. It brings me peace.

I drop a hand to her neck, relishing in the softness of her skin.

"Stop!" Riley pulls back so suddenly she nearly topples into the water. I catch her by the waist to keep her from tumbling in. "I'm sorry. I can't—" She looks me square in the eyes, that familiar tension returning. My stomach twists in knots as what she might confess. "I might be pregnant."

CHAPTER 7

Riley

My heart stops beating for an alarming number of seconds as Zac stares at me in disbelief. It's unsettling for many reasons. But the biggest is that I'm afraid I've ruined any chance of whatever was happening between going further. Going anywhere. *Way to ruin the moment, genius.*

"Pregnant?" he repeats, the word hardly a whisper as it escapes his lips. Lips that felt so damn good moving against mine only moments ago.

"It's a pathetic story," I say, pulling my hand away from his warm cheek. As badly as I want to kiss him again and pretend like I never blurted this embarrassing confession, he deserves to know what a mess my life is right now. "Boy meets girl. Boy pursues girl. Girl is fooled by his charms and gives in. Girl ends up the butt of a terrible joke."

"You don't know for sure?" he asks.

I let out a sigh, staring off across the creek. Hoping that some caribou might creep closer to the water and divert this mortifying conversation. "I'm too chicken to find out. I'm not exactly in the best location to buy a pregnancy test without half the town starting a rumor. I'd never forgive myself if Grandma Hattie had a heart attack on my account." The orthopedic surgeon I let charm his ways into my pants is very married despite his claims of a divorce being nearly finalized. Apparently, the divorce was complete fiction. A fact I learned the hard way when I caught him banging his actual wife in an exam room.

"What will you do if you are?"

"Good question."

"You're still going back to Orlando?"

I can't imagine anyone being thrilled to find out I'm carrying a married man's child. *If* I'm pregnant. Considering I missed my last period completely and I've been nauseous off and on, I don't consider my odds of *not* being pregnant too great. Grandma Hattie is a wonderful, loving woman. But I don't know how she's going to feel about this. I doubt she'll continue to offer me a bed if she finds out the details. I won't be welcome here. "I think I have to."

All I want to do is rest my head on his shoulder and drink in his warmth. Wrap his comfort around me like a blanket. Zac feels like the safety and reassurance I crave but definitely don't deserve. But I can't let him get tangled up in all this. It's too much to ask of anyone. "This is my mess. I have to deal with it, and I will."

"You don't have to face all this alone, Riley."

Damn the man for being so sweet and sexy all in the same heart-stopping glance. I pull my toes out of the water and hop to my feet. I can't stay here any longer. If I do, I might crawl into his lap and slide my hands under that too-tight t-shirt so I can feel those muscles ripple against my fingers. Even if Grandma Hattie locks me out of the house until her bridge night is over. "I'm a big girl. I've got this." *I totally don't got this.*

"Riley—"

"And no one knows about this, okay? Not Grandma Hattie. Definitely not Huck."

"I won't say a word."

"Thank you." There's something happening between us that goes beyond physical attraction. And make no mistake. There's *plenty* of physical attraction sizzling in the air between us. I'd give nearly anything to go back to his place and get naked with Zac Ashburn. To feel his hands roam all over my body. To taste every inch of his warm, hard skin with the tip of my tongue. To feel him inside me, taking to places I've never been. That earthshattering kiss is going to rev up the intensity of my naughty dreams tonight and probably many nights to come.

But until I know what my fate is, I can't drag him into my tangled web. He deserves better than to be caught up in my mess of a life.

"Is there anywhere to get ice cream this late at night?" I ask, certain there's not since Rose is at Grandma Hattie's.

Zac hops to his feet and grabs his shoes. "The gas station has a pretty surprising selection of Ben & Jerry's."

I'm so relieved for the normalcy that remains between us. Zac could be completely freaked out right now or ready to run a hundred miles in the opposite direction. Instead, that familiar bond of friendship reassures me he's not going anywhere. "What are we waiting for? Lead the way."

CHAPTER 8

Zac

"You sure you don't mind?" I ask my buddy Decker as we pull into Hattie's driveway unannounced. I don't have any idea how this'll go down. Riley might feel like I'm pushing her and hate me for it. But I can't stand back and do nothing. I need her to know that I'm here for her. That she can remove that tough-girl armor and allow me to lessen some of her burden. "Hattie Kohl can be a handful."

Decker smirks. "I'm sure I've dealt with worse."

We walk up to the door, but before I can knock, it flies open. "Zac, what are you doing here?" Riley glances at Decker. "And you brought...*company*?"

Grandma Hattie peeks over her shoulder, the same

mischievous twinkle in her eyes that she's been wearing since I helped Riley move the furniture. When I'm her age, I hope I enjoy life half as much as she does. "It's very thoughtful of you Zac, but you know I'm a happily married woman. Going on fifty-six years."

"Grandma Hattie!" Riley scolds.

Riley's shocked expression does things to me. Just the memory of her kiss awakens a part of me that I thought was permanently dormant. I wonder if she thought about me last night as much I thought about her. If she touched herself while thinking about me like I did while I was thinking about her. Did she imagine my hands on her body? My lips exploring every inch of her? "I *did* bring Decker by for you, Hattie, but it's not a date. I don't want to get on Harold's bad side."

"Smart man."

"I need to borrow Riley for a while."

"We haven't gotten through all her morning exercises," Riley says immediately.

"That's why I brought Decker," I explain.

Her arms are across her chest again. I can't help but drop my gaze to the perfect tits she keeps trying to hide. "No offense, Decker, but I don't see how bartending qualifies you to oversee physical therapy."

"Before I started working at the brewery, I was a medic in the Army for ten years." The mention of the military makes me stiffen with unease. Vague images are all it takes to unsteady me these days, but I take a deep breath and shift my focus to the present. "Some physical therapy exercises are a piece of cake compared to what I'm used to," Decker adds. I notice he has Hattie grinning from ear to ear. But whether it's his charm or her approval of me stealing away Riley for the morning, I'm not sure.

"See," I say to Riley. "He can help Hattie run through her exercises *and* keep her out of trouble. Right, Hattie?"

"Of course, he can." Hattie agrees so readily I can't help but hope she's on my side. That she sees the spark between Riley and me and is trying to help fan the flames into something that will make Riley stay. "He's lucky I'm a married woman or that *trouble* part might be a stretch."

"Grandma Hattie!" Riley gasps again.

Hattie winks at me, reassuring me that, yes, she's on my team. Before Riley came back to Caribou Creek, Hattie wasn't shy about her opinions. She told me more than once that I needed to find a good woman and settle down. Even if Huck blows a gasket, at least Hattie approves.

"I only have the morning," I say to Riley, hoping that'll coax her from the house. "Have to be at the brewery after lunch."

"Don't just stand around everybody," Hattie exclaims. "Riley, go get your purse. Decker's got things covered, right soldier?"

"Yes ma'am."

Hattie narrows her eyes at him. "We'll have to straighten a few things out. But I think we'll manage just fine. See you later, Riley. I promise not to run up the stairs while you're gone." She crosses her finger over her heart. "Scouts honor and all that."

Riley is practically shoved out the door a moment later. Finally, the two of us are alone. I yearn to pull her into my arms and revisit that smoldering kiss from last night. But outside the possibility of a very nosy audience, I can sense her hesitation and hold back. "I'm sorry to ambush you," I say.

"Are you though?" It's the playful graze of her fingertips against my bicep that eases away the tension. The hints of flashbacks have subsided completely, allowing me to breathe easier. Or maybe it's just that Riley is standing so close that the morning breeze can hardly wedge its way between us.

"C'mon," I urge before I give in to the temptation and pull her against me, kissing her like there's no tomorrow. Before things get physical again, there's something she needs to decide on first. "I've got some fresh coffee in the truck."

"I could kiss you." She blurts the words before she seems to realize their impact.

"Again?" I tease.

"Zac—"

"I know. I know. That's why I'm here."

Once we're both in the truck, she looks at me. "I don't understand."

"Do you trust me?" I ask, reaching for her hand and squeezing.

"I've always trusted you." Her worried expression softens, that familiar twinkle reappearing in those baby blues. "That was usually my downfall, you know. If I didn't end up covered in mud or soaking wet from falling in the creek, I was stranded in a tree with an irritated moose on the prowl or—"

"I lured that moose away, in case you forgot." I wait for her easy smile before I broach the more serious topic. "I'm not going to push you. But I also know one of the reasons you haven't found out if you've got a bun in the oven is because you can't buy a pregnancy test without the entire town knowing by noon."

A mile from town, I slow for the turn onto the private dirt road.

LOVE ON TAP

"We're going to your place?" she asks as I follow the half-mile drive to my cabin.

"I didn't think you'd want to pee on a stick at Hattie's." My attempt to tease falls flat as her expression goes blank. "Look, you don't have to do anything you don't want to. You don't have to share the news with anyone—including me. I just wanted—"

"Did you buy it in town?"

I relax, understanding her reservation now. "Of course not." Unable to sleep, I got on the road at four a.m. and headed south to the nearest gas station large enough to carry such a thing. I'll probably pay for that early morning four-hour round trip midway through my shift at the brewery, but I couldn't sit still. I had to do *something* to help.

Riley reaches for my hand, her blue eyes shiny with gratitude. "Thank you."

I try to pretend that her touch doesn't ignite every nerve ending in my body. I've always considered myself a patient man. But with Riley Kohl, I feel time ticking away all too quickly. If I want to convince her to stay in Caribou Creek, I can't drag my feet about it.

I park my truck in front of the cabin, glancing her way before I open the door. Even with the reassurance that no one in town knows, I can tell she's nervous as hell. My hand cups her jaw before I think it through, my thumb caressing her silky soft cheek. "What you do is up to you, sweetheart. There's no pressure, okay?"

"Okay."

CHAPTER 9

Riley

I stare at the three different boxes displayed on Zac's kitchen island.

No pressure.

Right.

My palms are sweaty, my pulse erratic, and those butterflies in my stomach are drunk. Not silly drunk. No, they're about-to-throw-up drunk. Nausea assaults me, forcing me to grip the counter.

"Hey," Zac says, resting a reassuring hand on my shoulder. "If you're not ready, that's okay too."

I allow my eyes to fall closed and focus on the sensation of his touch. I breathe in his woodsy cologne, inviting the distraction it provides. If it's the only thing I accomplish before I leave Caribou Creek, I'm going to find the bottle responsible for making Zac smell so damn good. Maybe steal a t-shirt doused in the intoxicating aroma.

"I'm not ready," I finally say, my words quiet and wobbly.

I'm not ready to face reality. I'm not ready to find out if I'm carrying a married man's child. Not ready for everyone I care about to turn away from me. I never should've believed him when he told me his divorce was almost finalized. I should have been more diligent in finding the answers for myself before I succumbed to his charms.

"You want pancakes?"

I feel the tension in my shoulders ease as Zac slides his hand away. "Pancakes?"

"Pancakes make everything better, right?"

His effortlessly sexy smile erodes the rest of my dread. I stare at his mouth, remembering how perfect it felt against my own. But the untouched tests remind me I should keep my hands to myself until I'm brave enough to face reality. "Not hungry," I admit. Well, *not for pancakes*.

I move from the island, eager to put some distance between those tests and me. Though the only direction I yearn to go is right into Zac's arms, I force myself to travel in the opposite direction. I stop at a side table against the far living room wall. It's covered in framed photographs of men in Army uniforms.

I reach for one and study the picture that includes Zac, my brother, and a couple other GIs. "Wow, you *really* fill out a uniform."

"That was in another life." He takes the framed picture from me and sets it back down. The graze of his fingers scrambles my brain. He's standing close enough to blanket me in his heat. I shouldn't lean into it, but it's too late. My back is pressed against his chest, my neck tilted in offering, and my hand reaching for his cheek before I even realize what's happened.

Zac nuzzles my neck, his beard tickling my sensitive flesh.

I sink into him further, forgetting by the second why I'm supposed to resist him.

His warm hand slides down my arm and settles on my stomach, holding me in a way that feels possessive. The wetness pooling between my legs outs me. I like it. I like it *way* too much. A soft moan escapes my parted lips, begging him to kiss me again.

"I'm sorry if I pushed you," he says in a low, heated whisper against my ear.

"You didn't." I comb my fingers through his beard, willing his lips to find mine. "I appreciate what you're trying to do."

"I want you to know something, Riley."

"Yeah?"

"No matter what you find out, I'm not going to leave you high and dry." He doesn't give me a chance to respond because his lips are on mine. Moving in that seductive way that makes it impossible to think straight. I snake my hand around his neck as my bones turns squishy and hold on as our tongues swirl together.

"Sweetheart?"

A thrill shoots through me at the tender nickname. "Yes?"

He moves his hand to my hip and digs his fingers in. "If I move too fast, you just have to tell me."

In this heated moment, I can't imagine anything being too fast. I'm soaked between the legs, desperate to feel his hands on every inch of my body. There's a faint whisper in the back of my mind, reminding me that I'm supposed to stay celibate, but I drown it out with a moan. How long have I waited for exactly this moment? Fifteen-year-old me never dreamed up more than a sultry kiss. But in the years I stayed away from Caribou Creek, I never completely put Zac Ashburn out of my mind. "Zac?"

"Yes, sweetheart?"

"You have more than a cot in your bedroom, right?"

His low, deep chuckle has those drunken butterflies in my stomach all aflutter as they bump giddily into one another. "Why don't you come see for yourself?" He slips his hand in mine and guides me down the hall.

He allows me into the bedroom first. But I only have time to register its massive size and the too-small bed before he steps up behind me and wraps his body around mine. "Better than a cot, right?"

At this point, the floor would do.

I spin in his arms, draping my arms around his neck and inviting his lips back to mine. In the passionate frenzy, I end up against the door with half my clothes missing. Zac's shirt is gone, allowing me the pleasure to run my hands up and down his chest. Every inch of him is deliciously hard.

He leads me to the bed, tugging off my jeans before we fall onto the mattress. I'm left in nothing but my bra and panties, feeling suddenly shy around the first boy—now *all* man—I ever crushed on. He's hard, cut muscle. I'm soft, generous curves.

"Don't do that, sweetheart," he says, hovering his glorious body above mine.

"What?"

"Second guess your beauty. You're better than that." He fuses his mouth to mine as his hand slides between my legs. Stroking wet silk with just the right amount of pressure to drive me wild. I rock my hips against his touch. I love the way his simple words instantly renew the confidence I lost a few months ago.

Zac kisses a trail from my lips to my belly as he tugs away my panties. I gasp as I realize what's about to happen.

"I need to taste you, Riley," he says in a near growl.

I've never had a man go down on me, though I've fantasized about it a lot. To have Zac Ashburn be the first turns me on in ways I never thought possible. I spread my legs wider for him in offering.

"Good girl." He rewards me with a drag of his tongue through my folds. I let out a long, drawn-out moan as I sink completely against the bed. Becoming one with the mattress and pillow beneath my head as his mouth performs some kind of magic spell against my pussy. He licks, suckles, and gently nibbles my clit. His tongue carves its way through every fold, tasting every bit of me.

When his tongues plunges into my channel, I buck my hips against his face. Fuck, that's...amazing. His deep laughter vibrates against me, intensifying every sensation. How the hell have I gone my whole life without experiencing this? My eyes fall closed as I rock in rhythm to his mouth.

Zac scoops his hands beneath my ass, fusing his mouth against my pussy so tightly I'm sure he's cut off his oxygen supply. It doesn't stop me from fisting my hand in his hair and pressing him harder against me. He laughs again.

"Oh my god, you're trying to kill me with that rumbling laugh of yours," I mock complain.

"There are worse ways to go." Those are the last words he speaks before he intensifies *everything*. The pleasure happening between my legs is dizzying. My toes and fingertips start to tingle as I reach that magnificent edge of the cliff. As I soar over the edge, crying out his name, I'm certain I've never experienced anything quite like this.

It's like flying.

I never want to come down.

CHAPTER 10

Zac

I secure the front door lock of the brewery and cut the power to the neon *open* sign. Fridays are typically one of our busiest days of the week, but this one was insane. Dozens of tourists exploring Denali National Park took a bus to Caribou Creek and spent the day in town. Many of them hung out at the brewery from the moment we opened until last call.

"What a day, huh?" Wes calls out to me as I head back to the counter and wipe it down.

"Went by fast." I leave out the fact that I feel completely depleted me for fear my mild complaining will summon Ben from his cave. He's been tasking me with extra shit to make up for Huck being out of town. And I've been doing his bidding just to keep Huck from getting the brunt of Ben's wrath when he gets back. Doesn't mean I'm not still irritated that I missed hanging out with Riley last night because Ben decided we needed to clean the fermentation tanks. *Again*.

Riley invited me over to watch the live-stream concert tonight with her and her grandparents. But with how fucking tired I am, I'll probably be passed out before Penny finishes her first song. Time is going by too damn fast. How long before Hattie doesn't need in-home rehab? How quickly will Riley get on a plane and head back to Orlando?

Unless I can convince her to stay here.

"I'm checking out a house on Fifth Street," Wes says, pulling out his phone and quickly typing out a text. "Interested in tagging along?"

"Not tonight. Got things to do. And I'm wiped."

"Wiped, huh?" Wes lifts an eyebrow in suspicion. "You're falling for her, aren't you?"

Leave it to my middle brother to see right through me without any effort. He's too perceptive for his own good. Sometimes it's downright eerie. But I'd happily deal with Wes over Ben. "Don't you have enough rental properties?"

"Only three," he says, studying me too closely for me to believe he's going to drop the whole thing with Riley. "I like even numbers."

"So do I," Ben announces, appearing at the end of the bar to count the drawer. "Preferably ones in the green."

For once, I'm happy to see my grumpy brother. He's just the distraction I need for Wes to zip it. The last thing I want is for rumors to spread around town about Riley and me. Especially with Huck still in Anchorage. He'll be back Sunday, and I still haven't figured out what to say to him about his little sister. I haven't come up with anything that guarantees he won't give me a black eye. But it doesn't stop a grin from forming at the memory of licking her sweet pussy. The taste of her still lingers faintly on my tongue.

"We're always in the green," Wes points out.

"We haven't been in the red," I add.

"We've been close enough." Ben doesn't offer a hint of a smile. I'm convinced if he tried, outside of the schmoozing his job requires, his face might crack and shatter.

I can't remember the last time the three of us hung out and just enjoyed an evening together. Ever since we signed the paperwork to take over the brewery from our grandparents, Ben seems to have lost all his joy. It makes me question if we made the right decision.

Or if he just needs to get laid.

"You want to come with me to see a new rental?" Wes asks him.

"Can't."

"Won't," Wes corrects him. "You mean *won't*."

"I need to run numbers."

"I already did," Josie Bennington, our administrative assistant, appears at the end of the bar. She's slipping on a hoodie with our logo. Ben pretends not to notice, but I catch him stealing a side glance as she wriggles into her oversized sweatshirt. Though he'd never admit it, he's crazy about her. But he'd also die before he bent his own rule about dating employees.

"You did?"

"I emailed you the report," she adds, offering him a soft smile he pretends to ignore. Wes and I have a bet on how long it'll take those two to give in. Wes thinks it'll happen before the summer's over. Convinced Ben moves slower than a snail wading through molasses, I bet two years. "Did you need me to do anything else before I leave?"

Wes and I share a knowing look, neither of us missing the hopefulness in her tone.

"No." Ben pretends to focus on the register. "You can head out."

Her smile falls, but she gives a nod. "See you all Monday."

Wes waits until Josie has slipped out the front door and I've relocked it before he drills into Ben. "Dude, what is your problem?"

"No problem." Ben pulls the drawer out of the register and sets it on the counter to start counting.

"Don't waste your breath," I say to Wes. "He won't listen."

"You should fucking talk," Ben snaps at me. "I thought I told you to stay away from Riley Kohl."

I bristle at his commanding tone. Sometimes Ben can be a real dick. My fists ball at my sides, ready to defend Riley's honor. Ready to tell my oldest brother to fucking butt out. "When you stop lying to yourself about Josie, *then* you can talk like you fucking know something." I don't wait for him to bark back at me. I don't give him the pleasure as I grab my keys and head out, leaving half the bar counter for him to clean.

It's not as if I don't know this whole situation with Riley is fragile. There are so many road blocks in the way of a happy future together. But unlike my brother, I'm not afraid to face them head on.

I'm falling for Riley Kohl.

For the first time in weeks, I wasn't stirred awake last night from nightmares. No, just the raging hard on she gave me in my dreams. I'm falling for her, whether I like it or not. Whether anyone else likes it or not. The way she kissed me back yesterday tells me I'm not alone in this. The only thing that matters is how am I going to convince her to stay in Caribou Creek? Because I *have* to. I can no longer imagine a life that doesn't include her in it.

CHAPTER 11
Riley

My body hums as I park in front of Zac's cabin. Last night, he fell asleep on the couch with his arm draped over my shoulders as we watched the live-streamed concert with my grandparents. Never in my life would I have thought such a simple thing could feel so...special. Or that I would crave so many more of those simple things.

I yearned to go home with him.

But I settled for walking him to his truck and stealing some very handsy kisses in the shadows before he promised to text me after he got home safe. All night long, I felt his hands on my body and remembered the talented stroke of his tongue through my folds. The way his beard felt brushing against the insides of my thighs. Needless to say, I'm about to spontaneously combust.

I should be alarmed at how easily I'm falling into this fantasy life, knowing that soon I'll have to return to Orlando. As much as I want to stay in Caribou Creek, things aren't so simple. Even if Huck doesn't freak out about Zac and me, I don't know what I would do for work. It's highly doubtful the clinic could support a full time PT. And then there's one important matter that still needs addressing...

It's why I've decided that tonight, I need answers.

I'm going to stop being a chicken and pee on all three of those sticks just be sure, one way or another. I still haven't had my period, going on six weeks now. But the lack of morning sickness gives me a small bubble of hope. I'll love all my babies no matter what. I just don't want to be tied to Chip if I can help it.

I nervously knock on the door, uncertain if I'm feeling jittery because of the pregnancy thing or because I'm dying to climb Zac Ashburn like a tree. Grandma Hattie sent me on my way with a bottle of wine and a promise that I wouldn't drive home drunk. I think it's her secret blessing to get myself a fix of the hunky military veteran.

When there's no answer, I twist the knob and call out for Zac.

I hear the faint sound of running water, and step inside. It takes concentrated restraint not to shed all my clothes and join him in the shower. *Focus, Riley.*

I set the bottle of wine on the counter and pick up one of the pregnancy test boxes. If two pink lines show up, will Zac really stay true to his word? Though I'm incredibly touched by his offer, it's not fair of me to extend that burden to anyone else.

At the sound of footsteps, my nervous fingers drop the box. Zac waltzes into the kitchen, drying his hair with a towel that obstructs his vision but leaves every other delicious inch of him on full display. I try to be respectful, but my traitorous she-wolf eyes drop right to his most impressive part. *Is that thing legal?* He's half hard, which leaves my imagination to wonder two naughty things; one, what was he thinking about that aroused him, and two, how much bigger does it get? *Is it hot in here? It's hot in here. I should crack a window.*

"Riley, hey."

"Oh, hey." The words come out as a squeak as I busy myself with the kitchen window latch.

"It doesn't open."

"Oh."

"I need to fix that." I catch him wrapping the towel around his waist out of my peripherals but still wait a few extra seconds before I turn around. My cheeks are no doubt a deeper red than his kitchen towels.

"Grandma Hattie sent wine," I say, thrusting the bottle forward in an effort to draw his attention away from my sudden awkwardness. But it doesn't stop me from wanting to lick those stray water droplets from his skin. "Said it's not responsible to drive home drunk."

Heat flares in Zac's eyes as a devilish smile curls his oh-so-kissable lips. Lips that know their way around my body. I'm so focused on them that I don't realize he moves around the island until he's standing in front of me. "Probably better spend the night here then. Just to be safe."

"Probably."

"Riley, you keep looking at me like that, we won't get to the movie."

I reach a hand to his side, digging my fingers into his warm skin. The simple gesture pulls us closer and raises my internal temperature a thousand degrees. All I can think about is molding my body with his. "What movie?"

He combs a hand into my hair, tilting my face up. "You're cute when you're flustered."

"I'm not flustered."

"Your denial's cute too." He doesn't give me a

chance to retort because his lips are on mine. Fire ignites inside my body, roaring to life and awakening every nerve ending in one quick swoosh. I grip his hips with both hands, meaning only to pull him closer. Except, the towel falls away. As does any chance of Zac hiding his eagerness or my ability not to stare at his now fully hard cock.

"Oops," I say, feeling my cheeks flush. I bend to grab the towel and crash my face right into his length. I freeze, feeling foolish and turned on all at once. My forehead rests against his swollen head. I could stick out my tongue and tickle the base with the tip. I already can't think straight with Zac this close to me. But with his giant cock unleashed, I've turned pure hussy.

"Riley," he growls.

I reach for the towel, but don't grasp it before my tongue darts out and licks his shaft. A fierce tingling between my legs begs me to it again, so I wrap my hand around his base and explore him with up and down strokes of my tongue. "This is fun," I say, my words spoken against his cock. With the groan he makes, I can only assume the vibration of my voice is doing to him what he did to me yesterday each time he laughed with his mouth fused to my pussy.

I drop to my knees as Zac wraps my loose hair

around his hand, pulling it out of the way. I'm so fucking turned on by the way he grips my hair, as if he's going to control the situation. *Good luck, buddy.* I take his swollen head into my mouth and suck him like a lollipop. "Mmm," I moan purposefully to increase the sensation.

"Fuck, Riley. You're going to make me come."

"In my mouth?" I flutter my eyelashes at him, enjoying control I've never had when it comes to Zac Ashburn. My inner she-wolf has roared to life, and I'm loving it.

"Is that what you want, sweetheart?"

"Yes." I tease his head with the tip of my tongue before I suck him into my mouth again, taking in more of him this time. His guttural groan makes me so damn wet I can hardly stand it. As I pull my mouth away, I twist his shaft with my hand. With one quick breath, I take him into my mouth again. Trying to swallow him as much as I can. But dammit, he's so *big*.

I use both hands to help pleasure his entire length as I suck his cock like it's my life's mission. Surprised that for the first time in my life, I'm not only enjoying this, but turned on by it. Who knew giving a blow job could be so much fun?

"Babe, I'm going to—*come!*"

Hot ropes of cum fill the back of my throat, and I swallow every last drop.

When I stand, I find Zac leaning against the island and panting heavily. I have to admit, I was hoping to get laid tonight. But I don't regret a thing. For the first time, I feel like I've fully embraced my sexual side. What else could I explore with Zac if only I found a way to stay in Caribou Creek?

"That was fun," I say, playfully biting my bottom lip.

"Fun?" he pant-laughs. "It was fucking amazing."

"I'm a little sad I wore you out, but—"

"Wore me out?" Zac's eyes darken instantly. He tugs me against him by my belt loop and cups my cheek possessively. "Sweetheart, I'm *far* from worn out when it comes to you."

CHAPTER 12
Zac

"I—I should take one of those," Riley says, nodding toward the pregnancy test boxes on the counter, despite her roaming hands promising the only thing she wants to do right now is go to the bedroom. "Don't you want to know first?"

"Sweetheart, I already told you. I don't care what you find out. I'm not going anywhere."

"But—"

I silence her with a kiss as I slide a hand inside her shirt to get it off. I undo her bra and let it fall to the kitchen floor. I tug her against me, loving how fucking good it feels with her tits pressed against my bare chest. "If you don't want to do this Riley, tell me and we'll stop."

Her eyes widen in surprise. "I don't want to stop."

A devilish chuckle escapes my lips. "Good to know. Because I have some plans for you tonight, and none of them involve sleeping." I unzip her jeans and dive a hand inside, loving how the damp silk feels against my fingers. Remembering how she tasted as she came on my face. My dick roars back to life, ready for more.

When I lead Riley to the bedroom, she's not wearing any clothes.

We collapse on the bed, and I crawl up her body like a hungry animal. I gently press my hips into hers, resting my hardening cock against her belly. She combs her hands through my hair as I prop myself up on my elbows. I lower my mouth to a nipple and take my time giving it all the attention it deserves. Fuck, I could spend hours—days even—just exploring her curvaceous body.

Riley reaches between us, wrapping her silky fingers around my cock. There's nothing fucking better than the feel of her hand holding my dick. I groan against her nipple, sucking in a breath to keep myself under control.

"There's a condom in my nightstand drawer," I say to Riley. "Can you grab it?"

There's a flicker of disappointment in her eyes I don't quite understand, but she reaches for the foil packet before I can figure out what's wrong. "Want me to put it on?" she asks, biting her lower lip.

"Go ahead, sweetheart." What I really want is to plunge my cock inside her without a rubber. But I won't risk knocking her up and adding another complication to her life. Not until we know what those tests in the kitchen have to say. Of course, the second we know I'm fucking her with nothing in between us. I'm claiming what's mine. But I have to admit, there's something erotic about watching her roll the rubber onto my cock.

I sit back on my heels and tug her hips toward me, spreading her legs for my viewing pleasure. "What a pretty pussy." I yearn to drag my tongue through her folds, if only to taste her again. But I want to watch her as I bring her to her climax. I slide a finger through her folds, pressing against her clit. "So fucking *wet*."

"That's your fault, by the way. I've been this way for *days*!" She moans the last word, her voice jumping an octave as I hook a finger into her channel and search for the spot that I know will drive her wild. Her high-pitched whimpers tell me I've found it.

I plunge in a second finger, using my other hand to give some much-needed attention to her swollen button. Every movement is slow but deliberate. I don't want to rush anything with Riley Kohl. I wish I had a lifetime to learn every little thing that turns her on and brings her pleasure, but I know it's not guaranteed.

"Oh my *god!*" she practically sings, rocking her hips faster to urge me to pick up the pace. "I—I—I'm going to—"

"Let go, sweetheart. I promise to keep you safe."

She surrenders to my promise, exploding seconds later. Her body shudders hard against my hands as she comes. She cries out my name loud enough to scare off the wildlife. I don't let go until she stops jerking.

I give her a few seconds to catch her breath, but no more. I pull her hips closer to mine and line my cock up at her entrance. She bites down on her bottom lip as her expression lights up. "Finally," she says as I push my swollen head into her slit.

"Fuck," I groan. "You're so fucking *tight*." I shackle her hips to control the motion, filling her inch by inch. I pull out slowly between each plunge, but it's torture when all I want to do is fuck her senseless. She must read the agony in my expression.

"I'm spending the night, you know," she says, running her fingertips over my hand. It's all the permission I need to stop holding back. I bend forward, lining up our bodies, and thrust in and out of my sweetheart like it's the most important mission of my life. She holds on tight, letting out a chorus of sexy noises as I pummel her pussy over and over. The bed frame creaks and all the blankets fall to the floor. But I don't dare slow down.

She comes the moment my dick starts to pulse. The sensation of her pussy convulsing around me is all it takes for me to lose control. I thrust one final time, holding myself as deep inside her as I can go and release my seed. The only thing that would make this moment more perfect is if the condom wasn't between us. The need to claim Riley for my own is overwhelming. I won't be sated until I can come in this tight pussy and stake my claim.

CHAPTER 13
Riley

I wake naked and wrapped in Zac's arms. There is literally nothing better than this feeling. Well, except the feeling of him inside me. I thought his cock might split me in two, but instead, it took me to one pleasureful euphoria after another. Heights that I never knew existed. Over and over. It's a wonder my legs aren't completely numb.

It's a bigger wonder that wetness drips down the inside of my thighs as the feel of his hard cock presses against my back.

I'm sore in the best way.

I should be exhausted.

But instead, I'm insatiable.

I lift my thigh up and over his leg, pulling his cock between my legs from behind. I spread my folds and press him against my pussy, rocking my hips in just the right motion to drive me crazy.

"Mmm." His warm hand slides down my shoulder and wedges beneath my arm until he has a handful of boob. He reaches around me to grab the other. As I use his cock as my personal toy, Zac kneads my boobs with his rough, calloused hands. "You're so fucking *wet*."

"*Still* your fault." I take my time stroking my pussy against his cock. Pushing his fat head against my clit and wiggling it around. I've never done this before. Never felt brave enough with anyone. But Zac has broken through all my walls. He's not only okay with me being *me*, he's turned on by it.

"That's it, sweetheart. Come on my dick. I'm going to come with you."

I rock my hips harder, using my palm to press him firmly against me. We gyrate together as he continues to tease my boobs and nuzzle my neck. The sensation of his beard against my skin reminds me how it felt between my thighs. That quick image is all it takes for me to lose it. I cry out his name as my hips jerk violently against him. Seconds later, he comes in my hand.

When we've both caught our breath, he nibbles my earlobe. "Soon sweetheart, I'm coming in that pussy of yours without anything between us." His heated promise causes shivers on anticipation.

I'm on the pill. All I need to know is whether or not I'm pregnant.

Familiar dread fills me.

What if I am?

It's one thing for Zac to say he'll stick by me. Quite another to follow through.

"I'm going to start a pot of coffee." He kisses my forehead. "Want me to bring you a cup?"

I *should* get up and get this whole peeing on a stick thing over with. But the temptation to steal a few more minutes in his bed, memorizing his scent, wins. "That would be great."

He turns my face with a single finger, drawing me in for a kiss that nearly makes me forget my name. I lost count of how many times I came last night. How many times we went at it. The night was a long, continuously erotic fantasy. "I'll be back."

He pushes off the bed and struts to the door buck naked.

Even his ass is perfect.

Of course it is.

I pull the covers over me and inhale deeply. If it's the last thing I do, I'm finding out what the name of his cologne is. A yawn escapes, coaxing me to stay in bed. Well, maybe I'll search his bathroom after a quick nap.

I give in to the urge to sleep, hoping Grandma Hattie's staying out of trouble. Grandpa Harold promised he'd look after her this morning since the shop is closed on Sundays. They're no doubt at the early church service. The thought makes me smile. I want what they have. Over fifty years together and still going strong.

Can Zac and I really have that?

It's the sound of my brother's voice that disrupts my otherwise perfect morning. "Did you get my sister *pregnant*?"

CHAPTER 14

Zac

"It's not what you think, Huck." His instant anger is understandable considering three pregnancy test boxes sit unopened on my kitchen island. That Riley's clothes are all over the floor doesn't help my case any.

"You fucking knocked her up?" Huck looks mad enough to punch a wall. Or my jaw. One swing and I'll no doubt lose a couple of teeth. If I'd known he was going to get back from Anchorage this early, I would've made sure Riley was gone. This isn't how I wanted him to find out. I wanted to talk to him, man to man. To let him know my true intentions with his sister.

"Huck," Penny warns, getting through to him like

no one else can when he's upset. It's the same way Riley keeps me grounded.

Huck turns to his wife. "Do you have another explanation?"

Riley appears in the kitchen wearing nothing more than one of my t-shirts. It comes down to her knees. If this moment wasn't so fucking tense, I'd tell her she looks damn cute in it. But that comment would definitely earn me a black eye.

"He didn't get me pregnant you idiot," Riley says, marching toward the coffee pot and pouring herself a cup.

"Huck, do the math," Penny adds. "Riley hasn't been in town that long."

Riley sucks in a deep breath that lifts her shoulders. I resist the urge to draw her into my arms, hoping not to poke the angry bear named Huck. Worse than him finding out we've been sleeping together is that the pregnancy tests are out in the open. The one secret she trusted me to keep is exposed thanks to me.

"Do you want to explain this?" Huck asks Riley, sounding more like an angry, protective father than a compassionate, caring brother.

"Huck, calm down," I plead.

He glares at me hard enough to shut me up. It's a look that promises he'll deal with me later. My heart thunders in my ears at the heavy tension in the room. Flashes from Afghanistan try their damnedest to get in my head. It takes every ounce of fight to keep myself grounded in the present.

"Are you okay?" Riley asks me in a whisper.

I give a terse nod, laying my palm flat against the counter. I focus on the cool granite against my skin. *I'm at home. In Caribou Creek. In my house. In my kitchen.* I allow the hard surface in my kitchen to center me. To reassure me I'm not in a warzone anymore. I need to stay present to defend the woman I love.

"Riley?" Huck asks, his tone growing more impatient by the moment.

Riley touches her soft hand to my bicep for several seconds before she passes by me and all my senses distill into one. Her warmth. Her touch. Her smell. Like my whole damn world has been washed clean after a spring rain.

It's *her*, I realize. She's the reason I haven't been having nightmares. I figured out they started up again after Decker got to town. We served a tour in Afghanistan together, and it was brutal. Seeing him after all these years has unexpectedly triggered some bad memories. He and I went through a lot of bad shit together.

But it's Riley who's kept me grounded.

"I don't know if I'm pregnant," Riley explains to Huck and Penny. "I've been too afraid to find out. And before you start lecturing me or shooting questions at me like a firing squad, let me at least get dressed." She gathers her clothes from the floor and disappears into the bathroom.

"You knew?" Huck practically growls at me.

"She only told me a couple of days ago. I was trying to help."

"By *sleeping* with her?"

"I care about her." I love her, but I'm not about to let Huck be the first person to hear those words. "I'm not just fooling around. I want to build something real with her."

"She doesn't live here, in case you forgot," Huck fires back. "And I doubt you're moving to Florida."

"Would you two stop fighting?" Riley snaps, her tone exasperated. The lack of sleep shows at the corners of her tired eyes. I want to tell everyone to fuck off and take Riley back to bed. Cradle her in my arms and let her get some solid sleep before she faces the shit-show she doesn't deserve. But Huck won't let this rest until the truth is out.

"Riley, why didn't you tell me?" Huck asks, his tone gentler.

"Tell you that I might be knocked up by a married man? Yeah, I'm sure *that* would've gone over real well."

Her words hit me like a sharp slap to the face. A *married* man? There has to be a mistake. Riley wouldn't...would she? The room feels like it's spinning. The faint echoes of another time and place grow louder in my ears. I try my damnedest to ignore them because I need her to clear this up. *Not the fucking time, PTSD. You asshole.* "You didn't tell me that part," I say, my words hardly above a whisper.

"Fuck, Riley. You were screwing a married guy?" Huck runs a hand through his hair, messing it up.

"An orthopedic surgeon I worked with, if you must know. One who isn't the best at keeping his pants above his ankles." She turns to face me, her eyes shiny with tears. "He lied to me. Not that it really matters, does it?" Her eyes fall to the tests on the island counter. "I might be carrying his child. I told you; you don't want any part of this. I should've pushed you away."

I feel myself unraveling from the inside out. The stress of the situation has triggered my PTSD more than I realized. I feel the familiar symptoms from years ago creeping back in. In minutes, I might put everyone in harm's way and have no control over it. I need to get help. Again. But first, I need to make sure everyone is safe. "Get out," I shout. "Everyone. Out!"

"Zac—"

"*Go*, Riley."

"It's not what you think," she says, her words fragile.

It makes me feel like a complete asshole to turn her away, but I'll never forgive myself if I do something to harm anyone in this room. I need everyone gone so I can calm the fuck down. The fucked-up circus happening in my kitchen is overwhelming my senses. I need solitude to get myself under control. "Everyone get the fuck out now!" I yell the words to get the point across, and finally, they go.

CHAPTER 15
Riley

"Whatever's wrong, it's nothing that a slice of blueberry pie won't fix," Grandma Hattie says, carrying a plate to the kitchen table and setting it in front of me. The twinkle that's pretty much resided in her eyes since the night Zac came over to help move her quilting room downstairs has faded, along with my hopes of a future with him.

"Thanks, Grandma Hattie."

I pick up the fork and prepare to eat my feelings. *Zero regrets.* At least about the pie.

I should've been honest with Zac from the first. If only I'd confessed the whole truth after that toe-curling kiss, I might've saved myself from completely falling in love. From conjuring crazy secret schemes that involved moving to Caribou Creek and potentially finding a new career. From getting my hopes up that Zac and I had a real future together.

Grandma Hattie takes a seat next to me and covers my free hand with hers. "You wanna talk about it?"

"Not really." I let out a heavy sigh. "But you deserve better than confusing silence."

"Oh good. You came to that conclusion on your own. I thought I was going to have to attempt the stairs to get you to spill the beans."

I laugh for the first time in hours. I've missed Grandma Hattie so much. Though I talk to her on the phone at least once a week, it's not the same as spending time with her in person. In a couple of weeks, she won't need me anymore. The thought saddens me. These are moments I'll never get back. "I may have made some less than ideal choices back in Orlando," I admit, hoping my confession doesn't give my sweet, albeit mischievous, grandma a heart attack. I shovel in a hefty forkful of pie and take my time chewing and swallowing before I add, "I let an orthopedic surgeon seduce me. A *married* one."

"Oh dear."

"In my defense, I believed the jackass when he lied

and told me his divorce was almost finalized. But that doesn't excuse my behavior. I should've known better. I should've seen through him."

"Bet he was quite the charmer," Grandma Hattie muses.

"He's better at that than being a doctor," I mutter.

Grandma Hattie chuckles, and I find myself relaxing. I thought I'd scandalize her. Well, I still might when I finish this confession.

"I haven't had my…cycle—"

"Period. You can say the word, dear. I may be old, but I'm not a total prude. If I told you what your grandpa and I were up to last night—"

I hold up a hand, effectively silencing here. "TMI, Grandma Hattie."

"You're pregnant?" she guesses.

"I don't know. I've been too chicken to find out. I'm a couple weeks late." She squeezes my hand tight, offering comfort I don't deserve. "It could be stress," I say. "Or—" I look down at my belly, "—a baby."

"Does Doctor Man Whore know?"

I nearly spit out my bite of blueberry pie. I should know better than to eat in Grandma Hattie's presence. "No. Contrary to what he told me, he's *very* married. I don't want to complicate things. His wife is a little scary."

"Well, if she murders him in his sleep, that's not *your* fault. He's the one who couldn't keep his man snake in his pants." Another bite gets stuck in my throat. Grandma Hattie pushes up from her chair to fetch me a glass of water on account of my repeated choking.

I set down my fork, giving up on the eating until I have some alone time. "Man snake, Grandma Hattie?"

That familiar twinkle reappears in her eyes. "I won't tell you what else I call it."

"Thank for you that," I mumble under my breath.

"No matter what you find out, you know you have a home here, right?"

"Really?"

She drops both hands on my shoulders and squeezes, resting her head atop mine. "Of course, Riley. We'd never kick you out. That punishment is too easy. It's much more fun making you deal with me when I'm cranky." She plants a kiss on my head and moves around the table to the sink. "I was talking to Mary Lou yesterday. Sounds like they might be looking for a part time physical therapist at the clinic."

"Really?" Part time won't pay the bills, but it *is* something.

"You want to tell me what happened with Zac? Obviously, you didn't get drunk last night."

"Not on wine." My smile quickly fades when the memory of him shouting fills my head. I'd never seen him like that. So stressed and on the verge of losing control. How could I have known one detail would upset him so much and make him take back his promise? We haven't seen each other in fourteen years. Maybe the boy I once knew has completely changed into a stranger.

"Oh, sweetie. He'll come around."

"Doubtful."

"He loves you."

"How do you know that?" I feign nonchalance, but my pulse races with undeserved hope that Grandma Hattie knows something I don't.

Before she can answer, there's a knock on the kitchen door. But Grandma Hattie isn't out of her seat before a bunch of people burst inside. Huck, Penny, and Zac file inside. I take a quick scan of the boys, surprised neither one is sporting a shiner. In fact, they seem to be...getting along?

I stare at the pie, certain I'm hallucinating. *What is in this?*

"I'm sorry I overreacted," Huck says, dropping his hand on my shoulder and squeezing. "You didn't deserve that."

"I did."

LOVE ON TAP

Huck steals my fork, so I offer up my half-eaten pie. As delicious as it is, it's proven to be a choking hazard this afternoon. I pretend to focus on the plate's blue flower border, but it's no use. Zac catches my glance more than once. He shouldn't even be here. He should be at the brewery working.

"I'm sorry for how I acted this morning," he says, nudging Huck out of the way to stand closer to me. He slides into the chair opposite me and turns it to face me. Our knees brush as he reaches for my hand. I don't realize I'm shaking until he caresses my hand with his thumb. "I have secrets of my own. I didn't come back from Afghanistan unscathed. I had a pretty severe case of PTSD. I got help for it. I thought I was through the worst of it and knew how to handle the rest. But this morning..." He squeezes my hand. "I made an appointment to address my recent issues."

I'm stunned to silence.

This whole time, I thought he was pissed at *me*. Replaying the events of this morning, remembering how out of it he seemed in moments, it all locks into place. The chaotic situation overwhelmed him. "You sent us away to protect us?"

"It was a precaution. If anything had happened to you—"

"But it didn't."

"Huck, Penny," Grandma Hattie says with a wave. "I want to give you something. And these two clearly need a minute."

We wait until the kitchen is clear. "Can I come with you?" I ask. "To your appointment? I want to know how to help."

"You already help more than you know." He cups my cheek and I melt into his touch. This is a hand I know would never touch me in harm. I know it in the depths of my soul. We belong together. I think we were always meant to find our way back to each other. To build on the foundation of childhood friendship with love. "Since I kissed you, I haven't had the nightmares. You bring me peace."

"Except earlier," I mutter.

"Well, that had some extenuating circumstances. But that's why I made the appointment. If you want to come with me, you're more than welcome." He pulls me closer still. "I want a future with you, Riley. No matter what the stick says. You're it for me." He sets a shopping bag on the table. "If you're ready, I'd really like to know the answer."

"That eager, huh?"

He leans closer, until our cheeks touch. His lips tickle my ear as he whispers, "As soon as you know the answer, I plan to take you home and fuck you with nothing between us. I'm claiming you for my own, Riley Kohl. No matter what you find out. You're mine." He kisses a trail to my lips, leaving me dizzy and breathless when he's finished.

It's time.

CHAPTER 16

Zac

It takes all my restraint, and several deep breaths, to stay seated on the couch with everyone else. Penny and Hattie gush over a baby blanket while Huck and Harold talk about some old car they want to fix up together. But my mind is racing too much to be a part of any conversation.

I'll take care of Riley no matter what.

If she's carrying a child, I'll help her raise him or her as if they were my own. I meant what I said. I'm in this for the long haul. But it doesn't ease the nervous tension not to know. Once we know, we can make plans for our future. I can help Riley figure out how to build a life here in Caribou Creek that makes her feel happy and fulfilled.

Finally, after what feels like hours but has probably

been roughly ten minutes, the bathroom door bursts open. "*Not* pregnant!" Riley announces, holding up all three tests. Her smile is filled with relief. A collective sigh fills the room. Grandma Hattie clutches her chest. There's a twinkle in Riley's eyes that's reserved for me.

I give the women a few moments to gab before I gently take Riley's hand into mine own. One simple glance causes heat to darken her eyes. She squeezes my hand in confirmation. It's time to make this future official. "Grandma Hattie, we'll be back later, okay?"

"You just found out she's *not* pregnant," Huck says, feigning disbelief. "Don't be trying to knock up my sister already, man." The room erupts in laughter as Riley and I head to the door.

Huck and I had a long talk after I chased everyone away this morning. As soon as he dropped Penny off at home, he came back to check on me. He was there when I was going through the worst of my PTSD years ago and knew how to help.

I told him how I felt about Riley. That I planned to marry her.

He admitted he wanted to slug me, but that was before Penny talked some sense into him. He left me with a threat to feed my body to the bears should I ever hurt Riley, which only seemed fair.

"I'm so relieved," Riley says as I speed through town.

"Do you *want* kids?"

"Of course I do." She reaches for my hand as I turn onto my private dirt road. Soon to be *our* private dirt road. "But when I'm ready. When *we're* ready."

We hardly make it inside the door before I have her pushed up against it. The urgency between us is intense. Our lips blaze hot trails as I strip away her jeans and panties. She tugs on my zipper, pushing my jeans and boxers to the floor. She fists my cock, causing me to groan.

"Nothing between us this time?" she asks, biting down on that bottom lip of hers in a way that drives me wild.

I scoop my hands beneath her ass and lift her up against the wall. She wraps her legs around my waist, guiding me to her entrance. "Never again, sweetheart. I'm coming in your pussy and claiming you for my own. I won't share you. *Ever.*"

She wraps her arms around my neck, holding on as she arches her hips against me to push me inside. "Good. You're the only one I want, Zac. I love you."

"I love you more."

"Not possible."

I flash her a wicked smirk before I pummel into her pussy in one powerful thrust. "I'm about to prove to you just how possible it is. Better hold on."

Epilogue
ZAC

About nine months later...

"Are you happy with *six* rental properties?" I ask Wes as I twist in the last lightbulb over the kitchen sink. His new tenant will be arriving any minute, which was a couple of days earlier than he expected. It's the only reason I agreed to dip out of the brewery early and help him to finish up a few things before she gets here. Well, that and Ben is being a total pain in the ass these days.

"Six is an even number," he says, as if that's an answer.

"It's a lot to keep up with. You're not going to hire anyone to help?"

He shrugs and squeezes out a sponge in the sink. "I like staying busy. And it's investing in my future."

"There are other ways to spend your time," I say, half ribbing, half serious. Wes hasn't dated anyone since he moved back to Caribou Creek a couple years ahead of Ben and me. He hasn't talked much about the woman who stomped on his heart, but it's obvious that it changed him.

"I'm working on a new brew," he says, as if that's what I meant. "But don't tell Benny-Poo. I don't want him to get his panties in a twist. You know how he is about change." Wes gathers the last of the cleaning supplies and drops them in a bag. "Thanks for your help, man. I'm sure your *wife* is eager for you to get home."

At the mention of Riley, a cheeky grin spreads across my lips of its own accord. "I have to pick her up from the clinic on my way home."

"You guys decide on a name for the baby yet?"

Once Riley officially moved back to Caribou Creek, we didn't waste much time. We were married within a month and pregnant two months after that. With my PTSD back under control and no longer wreaking havoc on my life, we decided enough time had been wasted during the fourteen years we spent apart. "Not yet."

"Liar."

"If I told you, Riley would kill me."

"Fair enough." Wes heads to the door. "I'm happy for you, man. Truly. Excited to meet my nephew, *Wesley*."

"Nice try."

"Hey, just remember, I'm the brother you like."

Before I have a chance to say something back, a rickety car pulls into the driveway. One I'm shocked made the drive to Caribou Creek. "Where did you say your new tenant was coming from?"

"Fairbanks."

"Good thing it's still summer."

A woman a couple years younger than Riley steps out of the car, shouldering a duffle bag. I'm about to tell Wes I'll see him later when I notice he's frozen in place and staring. Uh oh. "You know it's a bad idea, right?"

"Says the brother who was sleeping with his buddy's little sister and then *married* her."

I pat him hard on the shoulder, my way of wishing him luck before I head to my truck and leave the two of them alone. I recognize that stupid, goofy look on his face. I've worn it myself. He might not cave right away, but sooner or later he'll be in some serious trouble.

I head to the clinic, forgetting all about my brother the moment I see Riley step outside. With her six-month baby bump and radiant glow, she's never looked sexier. Some days I still can't believe I was lucky enough to snag her. Lucky enough to call her mine for the rest of my life.

"Hey, sweetheart," I say, greeting her with a kiss at the passenger side. She snakes a hand around my neck and yanks me down hard before I can get her door open. God, I love this woman so much.

"I'm crazy horny," she admits after she breaks apart the kiss.

"Good to know."

"Zac?"

"Yeah?" I open the passenger door and help her inside.

"I'm not kidding. I'm going to maul you the second we get home. So...drive fast?"

I don't even try to hide my wicked smile. "Anything you want, babe."

THE END

Bonus Epilogue
ZAC

Bonus Epilogue: about five years later...

"How long do I have to wear this blindfold?" Riley pats the silk sleeping mask covering her eyes as I pull out of the gas station. I've filled up the truck, bought enough road snacks to appease our entire family—though we left the kids at home with my grandparents—and insisted she pack an overnight bag suitable for any occasion. All to throw her off the trail of my real plans.

"Until we're out of town, and you can't figure out which direction I went."

"The highway only goes two ways—north and south."

"Pretty confident, aren't we?"

One corner of her mouth lifts. "I've had my coffee."

Life has been blissfully chaotic these past few years. We've had three amazing kids, Riley's been working full time at the clinic because Caribou Creek has proved it needs a physical therapist who's readily available, and business at the brewery is doing better than ever. So well that Ben no longer scowls over the numbers.

But in recent months, Riley and I haven't made a lot of time for just the two of us. I've been eager to get my wife all to myself. To remind her that she's still the center of my universe and deserves to be pampered.

Which is why when my grandparents told me they were coming to Caribou Creek to visit all their grandchildren, I convinced my brothers and a couple buddies to help me finish my surprise project ahead of schedule. Riley has no idea what I've been up to, and I can't wait to see the look on her face when she realizes I built a cozy getaway cabin near our special dock.

"Do I get any hints?" she asks as I turn on to the private dirt road.

"What fun would that be?" I tease.

"If I end up covered in mud—"

"No mud," I promise. "But I'm not guaranteeing you won't get wet. Very, *very* wet."

I roll the truck to a stop in the gravel area near the dock, pointing the truck toward the cabin. When I shift into park, Riley voices her immediate confusion. "Why are we stopping? We've only been on the road like ten minutes. I mean, I'm all for a pit stop if you want to get frisky, but someone from town might see us."

I take Riley's hand and squeeze it. "There will be plenty of time for *frisky* in the next twenty-four hours. Make no mistake about that." I lean over the center console, cup her cheek, and press my lips to hers. Savoring the taste of her. Taking my time as our tongues do a slow dance together.

When I break the kiss apart, I gently pull off her blindfold.

"What are you—" She gasps, bringing both hands to cover her mouth as she stares straight ahead.

"I have a surprise for you, in case that wasn't obvious."

"We're—this is—it's a cabin."

"It's *our* cabin."

Her excited eyes are shiny with unshed tears. For years, we talked about building a cabin along the water.

One that our little family could escape to on the weekends, or even just for a night around a campfire. A cabin she and I could spend some alone time in together without one of the kids screaming that another one hit him or stole his toy.

"Do you want to see it?"

"Of course I do!" She's out of the truck so fast I can hardly keep up. Halfway to the front door, she spins in a full circle, taking in the wooded surroundings, the creek our town is named for, and the dock where we spent so much time daydreaming.

"Even got the wooden rocking chairs you wanted," I say, nodding toward the covered front porch. It points west, her favorite direction, and I can already picture us savoring a thousand sunsets on it.

"It's perfect, Zac!"

I unlock the front door and allow her to go inside first. I try to rein in my own impatience as I give her a tour of the two-bedroom cabin meant to accommodate our family whenever the mood strikes. But when we make it to the master suite, the urgency between us crackles in the air. It's been a long time since we've been alone together outside of lunch breaks and naptimes.

"This is a *nice* bed," she says approvingly, slipping her arms around me in the doorway.

"It's a pillow top."

Her laughter is infectious. It warms me from the inside out. "It's like sleeping on a cloud," she says.

I comb the hair back from her cheek, tracing her jaw with my fingertips. "Wanna try it out?"

"You know I do."

She moves toward the bed, but I hold her back. She looks at me as if to say *what now?* "I heard it's better if you're naked." I tug her into my embrace, holding her tight against me as I crush my lips to hers. Her fingers comb through my hair as she moans into my mouth. My hands drop to her ass, squeezing her cheeks. Grinding her against me.

"You going to get me naked or what?" she asks between kisses, her eyes hooded.

I run my hands up her back, slipping beneath her shirt. It falls to the floor seconds later, followed by her bra. Though I'm eager to get to the bed and inside my wife, I can't resist suckling a tit. Not wanting the other to feel left out, I give it equal attention. All the while, my wife is stripping me from the waist down.

When her hand circles my cock, I make quick work of getting both of us the rest of the way naked.

We're a tangle of arms, lips, and all our favorite body parts as we collapse onto the bed. We roll as one, our hands and mouths roaming, tasting, and savoring.

There's nothing better than the way Riley feels against me, skin to skin.

"You like the bed?" she asks, hands framing my face.

I roll her onto her back and nudge her knees apart, lowering my throbbing cock to her entrance. "We haven't really broken it in yet." I push into her channel, filling her slowly and completely. Sliding home until our bodies meet and my balls graze her sensitive flesh. "Listen," I whisper to Riley.

"To what?"

"Silence."

"You're right!" She wraps her legs around my lower back, locking her body to mine with her ankles. Spreading her thighs wider and allowing me in just a little deeper. Fuck me, this is paradise. "No one's screaming or crying or tattling. Nothing's breaking. I could get used to this," she admits with a devious smile, running those soft fingers along the back of my neck and into my hair as I set a leisurely pace. I plan to take my time enjoying my wife every minute we're here.

"Sweetheart?"

"Hmm?"

"For the record, you don't have to be silent. Not even a little bit."

I drop my lips to hers as I pick up the pace just enough to make her whimper. Each thrust is deliberate. She rocks her clit against me every time our bodies join.

"Fuck, you feel so good," I groan.

She digs her nails into my neck, kissing me harder. Inviting my tongue in for playtime. Distracting me so effectively that I don't realize she's rolled us until she sits back. Hands pressed against my chest, tits dangling temptingly, and that wicked smile promising she's up to no good.

She leans forward only enough for me to take her tits in both hands. I knead and massage them as she sets a steady rhythm riding my cock. Each time she sinks down on me, she rubs her button against me.

How the hell did I get so lucky?

"I want you to come on my cock, sweetheart." I pinch her nipples at the same time, sparking her into action. She fills herself with me fully then starts to grind hard against me. Up and down. Up and down. It's the hottest fucking thing. "That's it, Riley. Make yourself come on my dick."

She comes apart seconds later, her pussy convulsing around my length as she lets out a series of moans that no doubt scares off the wildlife for miles.

It's been so long since we've just been able to let go and not worry about waking babies.

When she starts to catch her breath, I roll her onto her back again. She wraps herself around me like a pretzel and I thrust hard and fast, headed for my own release. I slam into her again and again, feeling myself nearing the edge.

"Come in my pussy!" she cries out.

Her dirty words cause my dick to pulse. I pummel into her channel once, twice, three times and still inside her. Shooting hot ropes of cum into her depths. Claiming my woman for what must be the millionth time since the first. Knowing there will be a million more ahead of us.

"I love you," she says, cupping my cheeks with both hands. "Thank you for doing all this."

"I'd do anything for you," I say to her, dropping a kiss to her forehead. "You know that, right?"

"Yeah, I do."

"I love you, Riley. Now and always."

I pull out and drop down on the bed beside her, still trying to catch my breath.

"You know something?" she asks.

"What's that?"

"The bed didn't creak. This thing is solid."

"Cedar frame. Pillow top mattress. I went for the best, sweetheart."

She draws me in for a tender kiss, but when she goes to pull back, I tug her right back to my lips. Crazy how a single kiss can recharge me in an instant.

"You know what?"

"What, sweetheart?"

"I bet you twenty bucks we can get this bed to creak before we leave." The mischievous twinkle in her eyes promises she's already up for round two.

"Twenty bucks, huh? You know this thing is crazy solid."

"Maybe," she says with a shrug, reaching between my legs and wrapping her hand around my cock. "But it'll be fun trying either way."

I have a hard time arguing with that. "You're on."

About the Author

Kali Hart writes short & sweet with plenty of heat. Instalove is the name of her game. She loves penning protective heroes with hearts of gold who'll do anything for the women they love. As a military veteran herself who served in the Army and completed a tour overseas in Iraq, Kali often writes characters with military experience and backgrounds. Because who doesn't love a good man—and sometimes woman—in uniform?

Visit her website: https://www.authorkalihart.com

Other Books by Kali Hart

Mountain Men of Caribou Creek Series
1. Love on Tap
2. Love Drunk
3. Tipsy on Love
4. Order Up: Love
5. Love Over Easy
6. Love a la Mode

Guardians of the North
1. Jaxson
2. Jordan
3. James
4. Jonas
5. Jasper
6. Joel

OTHER BOOKS BY KALI HART

If you're looking for bite-sized romances, check out these series:
> Brothers in Arms in Alaska
> Harrison Brothers in Alaska
> Stryker County Fire Dept.
> Stryker County PD
> Stryker County EMS
> Ryan Brothers Renovations
> Wilder Brothers Rodeo
> Reynolds Family
> Alpha Company Renegades
> Guy Next Door
> Rescued by Love

If you enjoy interconnected worlds in series:
> Daisy Hills B&B
> Heroes of Daisy Hills
> Holidays in Daisy Hills
> Bad Boys of Daisy Hills
> Daisy Hills Volunteer Firefighters

There are several others as well! Check out my website https://www.authorkalihart.com or Amazon author page for the full list.